DEFERRED REDEMPTIONS

Stories of Change

G. E. Russell

Dedication

This book is dedicated to my children, my nephews and nieces and grandchildren. The future is yours for the taking, show your brilliance and compassion in their fullest colors, it's who you were meant to be.

Table of Contents

Somewhere, Sister

G. E. Russell
2023

'Ding-dong-di-ding-dong, dong, dong. Ding-dong-di-ding-dong-dong'. The microchip's notes lilted ever so lightly over Esperanza Mejia's head, stirring her slumber. *'Ding-dong-di-ding-dong, dong, dong,'* chimed as she arched her back, opened her eyes, inhaling deeply. *Ding-dong-di-ding-dong-dong'* again, awakening her. Wiping her eyes with one hand, she reached for the cellphone on the nightstand. While bringing the phone to her ear, she pressed the bottom button, her dry voice rasping, "Hello?"

"Hello, is this Miss Esperanza Meh-ghee-ah? I hope I'm pronouncing that right." A woman's voice touched Esperanza's ear solidly enough to open both eyes wider.

"It's Mejia," Esperanza instructed, 'Meh-hee-ah."

"Oh, I'm sorry, hello, my name is Carol Shelton, I'm calling from the Colorado State Department of Education, am I speaking to Esperanza *Meh-hee-ah*?"

"Yes, this is she."

'Good, well, Miss Meh-hee-ah, I'm calling today because we learned from the University of Colorado that you're a graduate with a degree in education and have completed all requirements for your teaching certificate. Is that correct?"

"Ah, yes." Esperanza needed a sip of water or coffee.

"Oh, good. Uhm, well, the reason I'm calling, may I call you Esperanza?"

"Sure."

"The reason I'm calling Esperanza is, well, are you currently employed as a teacher?"

"No, no I'm not." Esperanza tossed off her sheet while lifting her upper body before swinging her legs over her bedside to sit upright.

"Good. Well Esperanza, the state of Colorado needs teachers. Having completed your degree at the University of Colorado, gives us an opportunity to extend a unique offer. Are you still interested in teaching?"

This question surprised Esperanza. "Uhm, yeah, I mean I'd like to but I don't have a license."

Mrs. Shelton continued, "Yes, I see that. But that can be accomplished if you teach in Colorado. Where are you living right now?"

Rubbing her forehead, Esperanza scrambled mentally to be sure of her answer. "I'm living with my mother in Arizona. What's this about?"

"Okay," Mrs. Shelton breathed into the phone, softly repeating, "living in Arizona." The sound of shuffling papers entered Esperanza's ear before Mrs. Shelton continued, "The state of Colorado is in need of teachers, especially those with credentials in elementary education like yourself. Currently, we have many openings in both Colorado Springs and Pueblo. We can offer you a starting salary of thirty-six thousand dollars a year and a new teacher recruitment incentive of an additional five thousand dollars payable over three years. Are you a homeowner?"

Esperanza chuckled at the question, "No, I'm living with my mother."

"Oh yes, you said that," Mrs. Shelton's flustering floated through the phone, "the reason I ask is we also have federal grant funds available for new teachers. Qualifying candidates could receive a one-time payment of as much as ten-thousand dollars for the purchase of a home in their district's community."

"Wait," Esperanza interjected, "You're offering ten-thousand dollars for a new teacher to buy a house with?"

"Im-hmm, if you qualify." Mrs. Shelton's tone became softer, less official. "Do you speak Spanish?"

"Uhm, yeah, I mean everybody in our house speaks it more or less." Esperanza wasn't certain how to explain how conversations or reactions in her family flowed between Spanish and English on a moment-to-moment basis.

"Could you could teach speaking Spanish, to Spanish-speaking children?"

Esperanza paused, "Well, I help my nephews with their homework and we all speak Spanish and English, so I guess, yeah, I can teach speaking Spanish."

"Oh, that's wonderful," Mrs. Shelton replied enthusiastically, "Because we can offer an additional thirty-five hundred dollars for ESL teachers. So, you could teach and realize over forty-thousand dollars for your first year's salary. Does that sound attractive to you, Esperanza?"

Esperanza sat still, mildly dumbfounded, someone was calling her out of the blue and offering over forty-thousand dollars a year to realize her dream of being a teacher. She silently wondered, *'Is this real? Am I really awake?'*

"Hello? Are you there?" Mrs. Shelton recalled her to reality.

"Yes, I'm here," Esperanza replied.

"Would you like to start your application process today, Esperanza?"

"Ah, I just woke up when you called, I'd like to think about it. Can I do that?"

"Well, how long do you need? I don't mean to be pushy, but today's June sixteenth and we'd like to fill all vacancies by August first. Would it be alright for me to call you, say, in a week or so?"

"Yes, that'd be fine. I'm sorry, this is kind of sudden, I'd like to sort through it, you know?"

"Sure, why don't you take down my information? Mrs. Shelton asked, "Do you have a pen and some paper?"

Getting up quickly, Esperanza opened her bedroom door and walked down the hall to her two nephews Marcos and Arturo Junior's bedroom. She bolted into their room, wearing only underwear and tee-shirt, going directly to their desk. Picking up a pen, she looked for something to write on. Finding nothing, she then went down the hall to the kitchen, where her sister Esmeralda sat at the table, drinking coffee, scrolling through her cellphone. Esperanza pulled a paper towel off the roll hanging under a cabinet. Laying it down on the counter, she bent over, pen in hand, "Go ahead, I'm ready."

Careful to not rip the paper, Esperanza recorded Mrs. Shelton's phone number and office hours in big letters and numerals of blue ink on the patterned white sheet. Once finished, she recited the information back. "Okay, let me think about it, and I'll give you a call, okay?" Bouncing on the balls of her feet, Esperanza nodded enthusiastically, "Yes, thank you! Good-bye."

Watching her younger sister's excitement, Esmeralda sat back, wondering what could be so thrilling at 8:20 in the morning? "What's that all about?" she asked.

Esperanza beamed, "The state of Colorado wants me to teach, they're offering me forty-thousand dollars for my first year!" Esmeralda smiled, nodding, "And what do you think Mama's going to say about it?"

The bouncing stopped, Esperanza took a deep breath and held it for a second. Exhaling slowly, she looked to her sister, "Hey, it's what I went to college for. She should understand."

"Oohh, she *should* understand huh? Yeah, well, let's see how that goes." Esmeralda's smile returned as she picked up her coffee cup and took a swig. Abuela Carlotta, the sisters' grandmother, had been washing dishes and listening, saying nothing, looking to no one, smiling to herself the entire time, just like she had every morning Esmeralda and Esperanza could remember. Esmeralda looked back to Esperanza, "Uh, could you get some clothes on? my boys' don't need to see your whoo-hah and fanny bouncing around."

Suddenly aware of her attire, Esperanza replied, "Whoops, guess I got carried away."

******

Gila Street in Yuma, Arizona, runs north and south, just west of train tracks and Redmond Center Drive. Beyond the tracks, to the east, twenty feet or so above in elevation, Interstate 8 begins its westward turn before crossing the Colorado River. Toward the southern end of Gila Street, a single-story building stands alone. It's a small restaurant facing west between its two entrances and exits to the parking lot. 'La Cocina Colibri' (the Hummingbird's Kitchen) holding six tables in its small dining area, is plain in appearance. Across the west wall, large glass windows shaded by extended eaves outside and a dark purple plastic film inside offer a view beyond the patio of the parking lot, trees lining the west boundary and a building to the south, across the street.

A simple concrete block structure, adobe walls surround the small patio outside the restaurant where patrons may eat at cement and tiled tables under tired umbrellas, washed and faded by the relentless sun. There's a smaller, streetside patio in the back where under Mexican roof tiles, a single table with five chairs accepts the ceiling fan's continuous effort. The only way in or out of this semi-secret patio is a reinforced steel framed screen door. The building's northern half holds a small, efficient kitchen having its own door. The kitchen opens Tuesday through Saturday at 10:00 A.M. sharp, the restaurant opens for business at noon.

Through two glass doors, customers walk only twenty feet to a counter holding a vertical glass panel. As patrons select their meal, tortillas, condiments, and sauces, they watch as it's prepared. Moving left to right, one person fills their order once it's selected. At the right end of the counter, before the cash register are stacks of paper drink cups, two sizes only. Next to the cash register, a space wide enough for a person to pass through and then a small stand holding a garbage container beneath the return shelf for trays and baskets. On a shelf underneath the cash register, a sawed-off twelve-gauge shotgun lies ready, just in case.

A dated beverage machine stands on a small counter along the east wall before the restrooms' doors. A model of efficiency, the Colibri is a little short on décor. The customers don't care, the menu is extraordinary thanks to chef Yesenia Mejia, an energetic woman many find charming and sultry. Her daughters, Esmeralda Del Aquino and Esperanza Mejia dutifully open the restaurant when mother Yesenia is away, although she always returns on Tuesday mornings by 11:00 A.M. to start the meats and beans. The three women work symmetrically, quickly preparing orders, cleaning tables, making change and offering pleasantries. Many patrons are local laborers, landscapers, truckers and others, knowledgeable in authentic Mexican cuisine beyond the normal traffic of Yuma. Some persons of questionable intent enter the rear patio to confer with Don Esteban Suiza, a solitary, middle-aged man who sits most days at the single table, out of sight.

"Esperanza! Where's the lettuce?" Esmeralda, 'Ezzy' as the family calls her, barks from the cash register. "I'm getting it, relax." Comes back from the walk-in refrigerator in the kitchen's north end. Stepping out with four heads, Esperanza or 'Espey' as she's known, cradles the vegetables as her hips push the heavy door closed.

"You haven't shredded it yet? What are you waiting for?"

"Ezzy, relax, you know how you get. It's only 10:30, you know they won't show up until 11:00, exactly." Laying the heads on the stainless counter, Espey takes out a large knife. One by one, she slams lettuce heads down on the counter, crushing the stem into the head before pulling it out in one piece. After four strikes, she rhythmically flashes the knife up and down, slicing each head into slight feathers of light green and white. In three minutes, the first supply of lettuce for tacos or, burritos or enchiladas is ready.

"What about the beans?"

"They're cooking."

"The rice?" Ezzy challenged.

"Also cooking." Espey looked up as the last head fell under her knife.

With admiration, Ezzy watched her younger sister, "You cut like you've been doing it all your life."

"That's because I have, since we were little, remember?"

"What's next?" Ezzy asked, wiping her hair off her forehead.

"Check the napkins, plates, sauces, enough out there?"

Flowing relentlessly from the west and south, the winds of June roll over the sandy terrain, bringing heat day and night. That doesn't stop the people who know and admire the menu of Yesenia Mejia.

"Mis pequeñas queridas?" A voice sings out as the kitchen screen door opens, "Where are you?" Mother Yesenia strides into her kitchen, her floral print dress flowing, red high heels striking the tile floor, her smile, lipstick and eyes all bright, happy. "There you are! Look at my lovely girls! Getting everything ready for me. Your father would be so

proud." With the kitchen being prepared, after changing into a pair of shorts and a tee-shirt, her heels exchanged for running shoes, Yesenia dons her apron and begins cooking at 11:05.

A sprightly forty-five years old, Yesenia is a beauty to behold. Many a man tries to watch her ever so slyly while she works the grill. They enjoy her dancing while cooking carne asada, Merengues' to the sizzle of pork or grilled shrimp, and sometimes a salsa step while preparing pollo al pastor. They may look, but Yesenia doesn't care, confident they understand Don Esteban's interest in her and his strength in silent, unseeable ways. Espey looks to the dual glass doors facing west and watches the silver Mercedes-Benz roll across the parking lot before turning about to park under the west boundary trees. That car, in that location, signals Don Esteban's presence.

Precisely at noon, Ezzy unlocks the double-doors to a line of men much longer than usual for Tuesday, then returns to the cash register. Espey smiles at the first customer, "Hello, how are you today?" The smaller worn man nods before firing off his order in Spanish and the day is underway. Espey takes every order, setting a plate on a tray or starting a meal in a Styrofoam container. The pace is quick, supplies are reloaded accurately by Marcos, Ezzy's oldest son, weaving between the counter and kitchen, keeping everyone's work flowing smoothly.

Shortly before 6:00 P.M. a white pickup truck bearing a large green diagonal stripe pulls into the parking lot. Immediately, six men in the dining room get up to leave. The Border Patrol agent walks to the double-doors and holds one open as the men file out. His friendly smile is ignored and he doesn't care. After they leave, he walks toward the counter, his eyes focused on Esperanza. He nods to the register, "Hello Esmeralda, how's things?"

Watching him closely, Ezzy replies, "Fine, Carl." The taller man looks to Esperanza, "Good evening, Esperanza, how are you?" His smile expands and his blue eyes shine. He's an unusual man for the area, his skin is a light, mocha color, and his hair a medium brown.

One might think he was Puerto Rican or maybe Cuban, but he's neither. He is Carl Ralston from Libertyville, Illinois. At six-foot-three, he towers over some locals. His arms are darkened by the relentless Arizona sun, but his hands are smooth, long fingers and broad palms, strong and comforting.

Espey smiles slightly, "Hello Carl, I'm fine thank you." This is their customary banter before he orders dinner. "What can I get you?"

"I'll have the enchiladas suiza dinner please," he looked to the kitchen to see Yesenia standing with a spatula in hand, staring at him. "Hola Señora, Que es esta?"

Hot from the work and the day, Yesenia snarls, "You don't impress me. Your Spanish is a cover." She returns to the carne asada, sizzling on the grill.

Carl's eyes go back to Esperanza, "Have you eaten yet? Let me buy you dinner."

"Carl, I told you, I don't eat until later, before we close."

His smile broadens, "I'm gonna keep asking, I want to take you to dinner. If you have to work, then we'll do it here." Espey likes his smooth style when he speaks, never down to her, like she is simple or naïve. Espey paused, taking in his good looks, his confidence, charms so rare in this small corner of Arizona.

"Enchilada suiza's platter!" Esmeralda yells to the kitchen, "Okay!" coming back sharply.

Carl stepped to his right, toward the cash register as Esperanza placed chips and salsa on the serving tray. Reaching to his back pocket for his wallet, Carl turned to the bells clanging over the glass front door, announcing more patrons. Watching the four young men closely, Carl left his wallet in his pocket. These were persons of interest to Carl, a group of young 'matons' or thugs rumored to be free-lancing as guides for immigrants coming from Mexico. Carl had no direct proof, but suspected Don Esteban was concerned these amateurs could make his life and business difficult.

"That's eleven-seventy-six," Ezzy said directly. Carl pulled out his wallet and produced a twenty-dollar bill. Watching Ezzy count out his change, he listened to the leader of the young men speak.

"Yo, Esperanza, you look quite beautiful today, how are you?" Joaquin Avilar grasped the top of the glass partition, pulling his torso up and slightly forward. His jet-black hair was pulled back into a small bun at the nape of his neck. A turquoise blue paisley bandana wrapped around his forehead, his slight frame and stature were more noticeable in the baggy black shorts and white sleeveless tee-shirt, his forearm's blue scorpion tattoo boldly displayed. Unimpressed, Esperanza replied, "I'm fine Joaquin, what can I get for you?"

"How about off this job and into my car, let me take you out." He smiled, his gold incisor tooth shining.

"No, thank you." Esperanza smiled politely, waiting.

"Which night? You know you wanna go with me. I'm the kind of man who can make you happy, very happy." Joaquin looked at Carl, his eyes narrowing at the gold badge on Carl's breast pocket. Looking next to Carl's belt, Joaquin spied the 9-millimeter pistol, "Hey, boss man, you ever use that?"

Carl turned to face Joaquin, "I'd rather not say," he replied, his face reducing to a smaller, professional smile.

"Why? You afraid to admit you shot somebody? Isn't that your job?" Joaquin squared as the other three stood behind, watching. Looking directly at Joaquin, Carl didn't blink, his voice lowered, "This isn't a conversation to have in the presence of ladies."

Joaquin paused, unsure as he looked first to Ezzy, who was staring at him with her strongest mother's glare. He looked to the kitchen to see Yesenia standing just ahead of Marcos, a spatula in one hand, the other behind her apron. Lastly, his eyes went to Esperanza's, her face just as stern. That look was the hardest to see, she was easily four, maybe five inches taller than Joaquin. Waiting a moment, he slowly brought his hands up as if to surrender, "Hey, chill out, everybody, I was just kidding. I'm not hungry after all," Joaquin conceded before turning to his associates, "C'mon, let's get out of here."

Pushing both doors open, the quartet left, walking into the hot evening air. The sun would be down in an hour or so, and then cleaning and closing the restaurant would begin. Finally, switching off the neon light signaled another Tuesday in the books.

✶✶✶✶✶✶

The night's darkness was occasionally pierced by random headlights shining down the street. Yesenia drove her older Cadillac carefully, keeping the speed limit, offering no reason for any authority to stop a car full of women. Marcos slept with his head on his mother's lap. Sitting in the front passenger seat, Espey looked to the sky, stars twinkling softly above the night's incessant heat.

"Mama, why don't you get the air conditioning fixed? Even now it's too hot." Ezzy whined.

"Do you know how much air conditioning costs?" Yesenia checked her rearview mirror, "Why should I put more money into this car?"

"Because it's the only car you got?" Ezzy was frustrated, this narrative happened at least twice a month, all the way to the house Ezzy and Espey grew up in. The house Ezzy briefly escaped for the seven years she was married to Arturo, Marcos and Arturo Junior's father.

"If your father had left me some money, maybe then I could have saved enough to buy a good car. But he didn't. He left you niñas and a pile of bills to pay. So now, I have to work every day, with no thought for myself." Yesenia looked again to the rearview mirror, her eyes flashing with annoyance at her oldest daughter's complaint.

"You couldn't ask Don Esteban?" Espey suggested to the stars.

"Don't you question me!" Yesenia snapped, "I'm not that kind of woman! I go with him for you! And your sister!"

Esperanza turned from the sky, looking at Yesenia in disbelief, "Mama, you can't mean that." She chided.

Yesenia looked to Espey, "What do you know college girl? While you were away playing games, I was made a widow! I had to make choices no woman should have to make. Who was going to help me? Your sister? Her boys? NO! I had to make these decisions alone, BY MYSELF! Nobody helped me, including you, Colorado college girl!"

The car's interior fell silent, buffeted only by the sound of tires rolling on warm asphalt. The women sat looking ahead or out to the side, but not at each other. As the wind blew through their hair, each one tried remembering when they weren't haunted by a husband's or father's death.

Arturo Del Aquino started a small auto repair business after he and Esmeralda married. Marcos would arrive in six months, and Arturo craved his son's respect as an honest working man. After many hours and careful attention to expenses, Arturo's Auto Repair became well known. Then local thugs, the *'Escorpiones Azules'* came and requested Arturo build extra storage compartments in certain cars. Later, they wanted extra plating, thick enough to stop bullets, built into the doors. Some vehicles had second gas tanks installed, giving the cars a range of almost eight-hundred miles. Despite repeated promises, Arturo was never paid for his work. After he refused to do any more until he was paid, he disappeared. Two weeks later, his battered body was found in a shallow grave in the Castle Dome Mountains.

Oscar Mejia, Yesenia's husband and father of Esmeralda and Esperanza, knew who caused his son-in-law's death and went to the police. They took his statement and thanked him for his time, but nothing ever came afterward. Oscar worked at the Yuma Territorial

Prison State Park where his movie-star handsomeness and smile were included in many tourist photos. Six-foot-two inches tall, broad-shouldered, and athletic, women compared Oscar to Ricardo Montalban, laughing coyly, flashing their eyes. Occasionally, Yesenia's jealousy erupted at some women who openly flirted with Oscar in her presence. Oscar laughed, his heart was forever given to Yesenia.

Four months after Arturo's death, a month after going to the police, Oscar's car inexplicably left the road and rolled over the bluff before dropping almost one-hundred feet into the Colorado River, south of Laguna Dam. Yesenia called Esperanza, begging her to return to Yuma immediately, but Espey completed her senior year at The University of Colorado in Boulder, graduating with a Bachelor of Science degree in Elementary Education.

The white Cadillac CTS pulled into the driveway on West 14th Place and stopped under a simple metal carport over a concrete pad extending from the small single-story ranch house. A wooden pic-nic table sat at the carport's back edge with two bicycles, a small propane grill and a plastic cooler. Behind, in the flat backyard of hardened dirt a lonely portable basketball backboard waited for the next shot. The house's evaporative cooler hummed through the stale night air, providing residents enough relief to sleep. Yesenia unlocked and opened the kitchen door under the carport to allow Ezzy and Marcos to enter. Holding him under her arm, staggering slightly up each step, Ezzy cooed, "C'mon *hombrecito*, just a little further."

A small stove light pushed the lad's eyes closed. Stepping to the entry, Espey looked to her mother, "Mama, I didn't mean to upset you." Nodding and sighing, Yesenia replied, "It's time for bed." After holding the screen door open, Yesenia followed Esperanza.

With Marcos and little brother Arturo Jr. sleeping in their beds, Esmeralda came to the bedroom she shared with Esperanza. Yesenia roused Abuela Carlotta from the sofa and the two older women shuffled to the third bedroom. After slipping out of her jeans and bra, while Ezzy brushed her teeth in the bathroom, Espey lay on her bed mentally replaying three years ago when Yesenia's phone call crushed her college senior year. The nightmare of her father's death, surreally retold through a cell phone, began the bitter family saga. She last saw him just before classes started, conference volleyball and basketball games, travel, finals, and dinners with teammates and friends. Now, all that felt like a distant fantasy, a faint illusion in blurred images and muffled sounds like a dream, believable but not real. Yesenia never understood a scholarship athlete like Esperanza had to make the team and play in order to keep attending classes. Yesenia disputed a college degree's value, worse yet, she believed it could make Esperanza undesirable. Occasionally, she'd mock Espey, saying, "I've never heard any man say he wanted to marry a woman because she was educated. You can be smart if you like, but you need to think about being sexy smart."

Walking into the bedroom, Ezzy asked, "Don Esteban? Really? You had to bring him up?"

"Oh please! Who's she kidding?" Espey returned.

"SSshhh! Keep your voice down!" Ezzy whispered

"Ezzy," Espey whispered, "When did she become such a saint? And for what? Weekends away from here?"

Tilting her head while lifting up one palm to her stop her sister's questions, Esmeralda closed one eye, "I don't know why. Maybe she thinks she's safe. Maybe she thinks Don Esteban will marry her, you know?"

Espey turned to her sister, chin down, looking up to her eyelids, "And do you think Ignacio's going to marry you?"

Ezzy's eyes flared, "Don't you look at me like that!" Her whisper was loud enough to be felt across the bedroom, "You have no right to judge me." Ezzy was incensed, the subject of Ignacio was a delicate one. "I do what I have to, to keep my boys safe from all those *cholo's* who come looking for you!'"

Crossing her legs before her on the bed, Esperanza replied, "So that's it? You think you're protecting your boys?"

On occasion, Ignacio and Esmeralda would accompany Don Esteban and Yesenia over the border to Mexico for an evening of dinner, drinking and dancing. Ezzy was expected to wear a red sequined halter-top dress of Yesenia's. Since both women wore the same-sized shoes, Ezzy wore Yesenia's cherry-red pair of four-inch heels. With hair and makeup done, Esmeralda was more than beautiful.

At the evening's end, after dropping Don Esteban and Yesenia off at Esteban's house, Ignacio would bring Ezzy home where in the dark of the carport he would sit on the pic-nic table, undoing her halter, fondling her breasts as she fellated him. Many late Saturday nights, Esperanza would awaken to see the red-sequined dress on their bedroom floor or hear the soft echoes of Esmeralda brushing her teeth in the bathroom before her muffled sobs of crying herself to sleep.

Ezzy rationalized, "Hey, everybody knows El Compadre is at our restaurant most days. They know better than to mess with his woman or her family, that family is us: you, me, my boys even Abuela Carlotta. I've got to keep my boys safe, get them out of here and into college. After they're set up, I'm out of here too."

"Oh yeah?" Esperanza looked to sister, a slight grin twisting one corner of her mouth, "You think El Compadre's okay with that? What if he comes after you? What then?"

"*Nenita*, once you've been with a man, you know what all of them are like." Esmeralda laid down on her bed, looking to the ceiling she spoke softly, "Even my Arturo, once that *pene* starts acting up, the blood leaves their brain. They'll do anything for your hand, your mouth, and your soul, to fix them. Anything." She exhaled long and slow, "You've got to know how to handle a man, be sure you get what you need before he gets what he wants. Otherwise, you're just a piece of meat."

"If you get that far." Esperanza now recalled the one guy she slept with in college. "Sometimes, you're just something to play with, you know?" Esmeralda turned her head to see her sister looking at the ceiling also, "You're thinking about that white boy playing with you in college, you couldn't see it."

"The way you can't see Don Esteban watching you in the kitchen?"

Looking back to the ceiling, Esmeralda stated, "Hey, he can look all he wants, if he tries touching me, that's different." Propping herself up on one elbow, Espey turned to her sister, "So, if he wants your mouth some afternoon, what happens then?"

"If he helps my boys get into college, I'll suck his dick, but first, he's gotta fix the air conditioning in Mama's car." Esmeralda looked at her sister as they both burst into laughter, covering their mouths, trying to keep quiet.

******

Thursday was exceptionally hot, even for Yuma, with the temperature climbing to 114 degrees by one o'clock. Lunch time traffic was heavy and the women worked furiously to keep patrons moving across the counter to the register. Under the table umbrellas outside, working men of all stripes sat eating, talking, wiping their foreheads with colored handkerchiefs. Marcos constantly moved between cleaning tables, washing trays, emptying trash containers and resupplying napkin holders, plastic forks, and spoons. Twice, he had to refill the ice cube containers at the beverage machines. After his second effort, he asked his grandmother, "Abuela, I thought you were getting a new machine? Where is it?"

At that precise moment, Don Esteban's driver and body guard Ignacio, entered the kitchen from the back patio door, an empty glass pitcher in hand. Looking to Ignacio first, Yesenia answered, "I don't know *Nieto*, maybe we should ask?"

She took the empty pitcher and went to the walk-in refrigerator, Ignacio closely behind her. It was his job to be certain she poured the lemonade from Don Esteban's preferred blend kept in the refrigerator, away from anyone's interference. Watching her pour from the large three-gallon jug, he said, "Maybe I could suggest your old machine is, struggling to keep ice?"

Yesenia's eyes brightened up as she smiled, showing her perfect teeth and one dimple on her right cheek, "Yeah? You would do that for me?" Her eyelashes batted quickly as she stared into his eyes. Ignacio smiled and nodded before taking the filled pitcher. Once he was out of the kitchen, Yesenia went out to the dining room, some people waited in line while many others enjoyed their meals. She asked aloud, "Okay, what's next?"

Espey turned first. Ezzy handed change to a customer before also turning, "We're kind of busy here, Ma, what're you doing?" Ezzy then looked to Espey before both turned their surprise back to their mother.

"Oh, I was just watching my lovely daughters," Yesenia laughed, "working so hard." Turning to Marcos, she placed her hand on his shoulder, guiding him back into the kitchen. "Come on, *Nieto*, let's get to work."

"Esperanza Mejia, come away with me, make me the happiest man on earth." The voice carried over the glass partition, hovering above the refried beans, rice, tomatoes, cilantro, and other condiments. Turning to the voice, Espey's disapproval showed, "Joaquin," She leaned on the counter, "what do you want?"

"I want to take you down by the river tonight, we can lay together under the stars, sharing our love."

"Uh-huh, and what's that going to do for me?" Espey challenged Joaquin directly, causing his three friends to step back, closing their hands over their mouths, like they were choking on her words.

"Esperanza, why you gotta do me like that in front of everybody? I'm talking about my love for you, my dreams for us, our beautiful children, you and me, we could make beautiful babies. Esmeralda knows what I'm talking about," he looked to her, "Don't you, Ezzy, you know how to make beautiful babies, right?" Joaquin smiled broadly as he pulled the toothpick out of his teeth.

Ezzy smiled to a customer while taking his debit card for payment, not looking in Joaquin's direction, acting as if she hadn't heard his question. A small receipt rolled forward from the device and she tore it off, handing it and the card back, "Thank you, have a nice day."

As the man took his bag of lunches and walked away, Ezzy stepped to her right, sliding down the counter until three feet from Joaquin, "Hey, El Tonto, shouldn't you and your friends be on the swings at the playground?"

The three amigos burst out laughing as Joaquin's face reddened. Espey covered her mouth and bowed her head slightly, trying to hide her laughter. Ezzy wasn't playing though, her fiery eyes stared at Joaquin, waiting for any reaction. Joaquin looked to Esperanza, his eyes wide, his jaw clenched, "Go ahead! Laugh! I don't care, I'm going to show you all how foolish you are!"

"Joaquin, stop." Espey chuckled, "We're just playing. Want do you want?"

"What do I want?" He looked around the room, "I told you, I want you, with me. What do you want?"

Now Esperanza took the lead, "What do I want? Hmn, let's see. You want to lay with me, no?"

"No!" Joaquin replied, "I want us together, I want to give you my babies." His smile grew, a shorter, Cheshire-cat-like smile as he watched her closely.

"Oh, you want to give me *your* babies huh? That's it, I get *your* babies? For what? Eighteen, twenty years after what? Five minutes of you pumping and jumping between my legs like a monkey, grunting and sweating? Uh, no thanks." Esperanza stood tall, her five-foot eleven-inch frame fully erect, shoulders broad, looking down at Joaquin, quaking with frustration and embarrassment.

"You think you're so much better than us!" He snarled, "College girl! Hah! What a joke! They take your money, and tell you a bunch of lies about how life will be better. Better than what?! You get loans you gotta pay back and still can't get a job!" His three friends stood silent, eyes searching to see if anyone else was watching.

Joaquin continued ranting, "They tell you to graduate high school and get a job. For what? Be a busboy at some restaurant? Work at Jiffy-Lube? For what!?" Three seconds of silence grew into four, then five before Esperanza sternly asked, "What would you like to order sir?"

Joaquin's body trembled as he growled in a low voice, "You think you're better than us cuz' you went to college. Look around *perra*, you right back here, just like her!" His eyes darted to Ezzy, "She thought she was something when her man was making all that money. What happened to him? Or your old man, what happened to both of them, eh?"

His glare returned to Esperanza, "Just like all the other *mula's*, you're only good for making babies." Stepping back, Joaquin spit on the floor then barked, "Let's get out of here."

As the quartet walked through the double glass doors, Esperanza saw her sister's shaking body, tears lining her eyes, white knuckles clenching the counter's edge. Ezzy stood trembling in a moment of no customers, no sounds, no escaping her reality.

✶✶✶✶✶✶

Friday's lunch crowd was a tsunami of hungry workers, bringing wallets full of cash and empty stomachs. Friday was payday for those who accepted work only paying cash at substantially reduced rates. They came to Cucina Colibri either to be told by Don Esteban which company to report to next week or to pay him his referral fee. Knowing their circumstances, the women made sure every peon got ample servings. Such generosity slowed the kitchen and order process but these women understood the hard work and that many small faces depended on that money for meals, clothes and rent. A hard-working man can do a lot of good on a full belly.

As the rush ebbed, the familiar white pickup truck rolled into the parking lot, clouds of dust billowing up from its rear tandems. But instead of parking near the front patio, it went directly to the Mercedes. The silver car was pointed south, the pickup stopped alongside, positioning each vehicle's driver-side doors opposite one another. Carl Ralston stepped out of his truck and knocked on the Mercedes. The black window rolled down as Ignacio looked up, "Yes."

"I need to talk to him."

"About what?"

Looking directly at Ignacio, Carl replied, "That's between me and him." The window rose silently as Carl stood with hands on hips in the blinding light and heat. A moment later, the door opened and Ignacio got out, "Come with me."

The two walked across the dirt lot, Ignacio in the lead, small dusty wisps flowing up behind them. Ignacio smiled to the air, "It's a hot one today, eh amigo?" Carl replied, "Ignacio, it's hot here every day."

"Eh-heh, yes, it is." His smile stayed wide as he looked left and right. As they approached the wrought-iron door, Carl knew to stop three feet away. Ignacio stepped forward and pressed a small white button in the adobe wall, to the door handle's right. After a moment, a buzzing sound released the lock and Ignacio opened the door. As Carl started to enter, Ignacio extended one hand, palm up, "First the weapon." Carl stopped and put his right hand on the pistol handle, "Not gonna happen."

Ignacio started closing the door when the voice from the shadows asked, "Why are you here?" In a voice just loud enough to carry twenty or so feet, Carl replied, "Don Esteban, I come with a request as a person, not an agent or a threat." Silence. Then the voice said, "Let him in."

Ignacio pulled the door open and after Carl passed through, Ignacio started to enter. Don Esteban called out, "It's okay, wait in the car."

Surprised, Ignacio stopped with one foot inside the patio. He waited a moment, then turned and left, walking back to the Mercedes, head down, annoyed at being reduced to waiting in the heat. Carl stood still as Don Esteban watched Ignacio's departure. The wrought-iron door had a sun-screen over it, from outside you could see nothing in the patio. From inside the patio, you could see the outside clearly. Carl noticed wrought-iron bars standing vertically between the corners of the east wall's hemispherical open space. Only six inches apart and also behind a sunscreen, visibility outside to Gila Street was easy. In the corner close to the kitchen door, the round table and chairs sat under a ceiling fan silently spinning above, its pull chain making small circles thanks to one blade's imbalance. Don Esteban sat in his corner chair, straight-faced, "You say you come as a person but you insist on keeping your weapon."

"Yessir, technically, I'm on duty right now," Carl answered.

"Then you're an agent."

"Not for what I'm about to say, sir."

Don Esteban nodded, a curious single eyebrow lifting up, his mind working. "What do you have to say to me?"

"I've learned some local, let's say, 'bad actors' are planning to intercept a group of immigrants, many of them women and children, crossing somewhere near and hold them for ransom or get them to sign over their pay."

"I work with men." Don Esteban firmly averred, "I have no need for women or children." Don Esteban calmly asked, "Why do you think I need to hear this?"

"I believe you, sir. I don't believe these boys work for you." Carl too, needed to be cautious. "That's why I'm asking you, sir, man to man, to stop this, to protect innocent people, especially here at the restaurant. Certain people here are special to me, sir, I don't want to see them hurt if I or possibly you, can prevent it."

Don Esteban paused, carefully weighing Carl's words. His face relaxed as a slight smile came forward, "Does Esperanza know you're doing this?" His smile morphed into a softer, more paternal confidence, "She's a beautiful woman, don't you think?"

Keeping his eyes level-set, Carl calmly replied, "Sir, I know our people take great pride in family and honor, the honor of our women being most dear."

"Our people?" Both of Don Esteban's eyebrows rose, opening his face with surprise, "What do you know of our people, *Chico Blanco*?"

"With all due respect sir, my mother came from Hermosillo, I'm half Mexican."

"Yeah? Do I know her?"

"I don't think so, she went to college in Tucson, then moved up north. She married my father in Chicago over thirty years ago. My birth name is Carlos, but I go by Carl." Carl had let his guard down a little thinking it helped, giving Don Esteban some special information.

Don Esteban considered Carl's admission, taking a long, slow drag off his cigar. Looking through the iron bars out to Gila Street, he spoke slowly, "I'm not aware of anything you say you *think* might happen. I don't know who, if anybody, might be foolish enough to do such a thing."

"Don Esteban, there are women here we both care about, they might be at risk sometime in the very near future. I'm asking you to do whatever you can to help keep them safe. Nothing more."

"And If I keep them safe?" Don Esteban took one hand and, starting at his forehead, ran it front to back all the way to his neck, "What can I expect in return?"

Carl remained strong, holding his position, "This is not professional, this is not our business. This is one man to another, asking on your honor, sir." Waiting a moment, Don Esteban searched the light outside the iron bars before replying, "I'll do what I can."

"Muchas gracias Don Esteban," Carl nodded and turned, walking to the door and out to his truck.

******

When Carl's truck pulled into the parking lot, Ezzy and Espey both watched closely. Ezzy always kept an eye on the silver Mercedes, Espey waited to see if Carl was coming in for lunch. Both women became nervous when Ignacio led Carl to the back patio.

"Ezzy, where are they going?" Espey asked. Her eyes open, her tongue silent, Ezzy watched the two men walk past the doors. A few seconds later, a call came out from the kitchen, "Girls, come quickly!"

Dressed in the same blue jeans and pink 'Cocina Colibri' tee shirts, the sisters rushed to their mother who was waiting by the grill, she asked, "What are those two talking about?"

Yesenia kept watching the kitchen screen door opening to the patio, Carl and Don Esteban being only twenty feet away, their conversation was muffled by the large kitchen exhaust fan. "This is not good," Yesenia pulled on her lower lip, "When men like these get together and talk, something bad happens."

"Ma, you don't know that." Espey hushed.

"Mama's right," Ezzy said, "Look, they're both serious, something's not right. These two don't see things the same." The three women huddled together watching until Marcos walked in with a tub full of silverware and plates for washing. "What's going on?" he asked.

Yesenia jerked her body up, "*Nieto*, what've you got there?" Lifting the tub, the boy innocently replied, "The dishes Abuela." "Okay, okay, girls, get back to work." She put a hand on each daughter's shoulder, turning them back towards the dining room. "Marcos, let's get busy here, okay?"

Ezzy and Espey returned to their stations, each occasionally staring out to the parking lot, not focusing on any one vehicle or person. Espey stacked more Styrofoam to-go containers under her side of the counter, Ezzy took a damp cloth and wiped the counter area around and in front of the register. It was almost three o'clock, there was no one eating in the dining room, only three men sat outside at one table.

Coming from the walk-in refrigerator with chopped onions and more pico de gallo, Espey noticed Ezzy at the register, her shoulders quaking ever so slightly. Placing the containers on the counter, Espey asked, "Ezzy, what's the matter?"

"God, I hate it here."

"Whaa? What do you mean?" Espey placed her hand on Ezzy's right shoulder, looking at her sister's eyes now lined by tears across their lower edges. Esmeralda was always the tougher sister, combative, unafraid, always protecting the younger, taller Esperanza. Ezzy had her mother's dimples, fiery eyes, shapely hips and bust at sixteen. Bold in her opinion, a bookend to her mother in personality and charm. Three years younger, Esperanza grew faster, taller, and bigger than her older sister. So much in fact, people often mistook her to be the eldest daughter. But the sisters were always very close, sharing a bedroom all through their school years.

Esmeralda graduated high school and immediately worked waiting tables at Denny's. Frequently, she'd make over three hundred dollars in cash, giving her enviable independence and spending ability. A year later, one Sunday morning around three a.m., Arturo Del Aquino came in slightly drunk and was immediately smitten by Esmeralda's alluring smile, fiery eyes, and feisty personality. After their marriage, Esmeralda worked in the shop as the bookkeeper and service scheduler. A single tear slid down Ezzy's cheek as she confessed, "I can't wait to leave. I'm tired of always being afraid."

"Afraid?" Espey was stunned, "Of what?"

Looking out the windows, afternoon shadows of table umbrellas stretching out across the patio tiles like elongated mushrooms, Ezzy voiced words and feelings long buried in her heart. "I never thought about what boys have or don't have here. When I waitressed, I lived at home, slept in my bed, partied with Lucia and Cassandra, didn't care about nothing." Espey returned to her side of the counter, listening while wiping with a cloth, "And?"

"They don't have much, but girls have even less." Sighing heavily, Esmeralda grabbed a broom and walked to an empty table. "Arturo's cousin Romeo has a body shop outside Atlanta. He got away from the gangsters, drug mules, all that shit waiting for boys here. He wanted us to move to Georgia and open a repair shop next to his. Said we'd make money easy."

Espey stopped wiping, "Would you go?"

Ezzy stopped sweeping, "Hell yes! We were getting ready when Arturo told the Escorpiones he needed to be paid." Ezzy looked back outside, reliving her hopes in the day's sunlight, "He said if they paid the five thousand they owed, we'd leave in a heartbeat. He said even if they only paid half, he'd make it work." Her chin quivered under the memory of their escape plan.

Esperanza stood still, "Did Mama and Papa know about this?

Wiping her eyes, Ezzy nodded, "They were sad, but Papa said he understood, our boys needed a fresh start." She looked out to the parking lot, "Then they took my Arturo made sure the police did nothing. Then after Papa complained, they got him. It's always the same, the *matons* are boys who have nobody showing them a different life. They kill everything they don't understand, then they kill each other." Ezzy's tears streamed freely as she alternated between sweeping the floor and wiping her cheeks. Her head down, some tears fell into the dust pile, accumulating in front of her broom. Sweeping and sighing she confessed aloud, "Goddamn, I hate it here."

Watching her sister's anguish, Espey considered how life for all three women had passed, changing them but not their circumstances. She recalled her mother pleading through the telephone for her to come home, *'Right now Esperanza, I need you here, not playing basketball somewhere.'* Espey thought to herself, *'Now we're playing a different game, but nothing we're doing is giving us answers.'*

That thought got louder as Espey and Marcos pulled the bag from the trash container by the doors. Stopping to tie the top closed, she looked at the worn tiles, the chairs, some bent and faded in color. Ezzy bent over and swept up the dust and crumbs and bits and pieces once more, as she had done the last three years, Tuesday through Saturday. Taking the new trash bag out from her back pocket, Espey asked herself, *'Where's that teacher you held in your heart?' The woman coach for girls who, like herself, wanted their own life? Where'd she go?'*

As Marcos struggled with the bulging bag to the dumpster, Esperanza remembered the last time she saw her father alive. It was their breakfast together at Willoughby's before she flew back to

Boulder for her senior year. As was his habit, Oscar requested the booth under the poster-sized picture of Esperanza shooting a free-throw during her high-school career. He would look at the photo occasionally and smile, his broad, movie-star smile.

"*Mi querida,*" He beamed, "This is your big year. I can't wait to see you graduate."

"Papi, stop." Espey blushed, "Why do you say that?"

"Because it's what you've been working for, right?" The smile beamed like a lighthouse for anyone to see. He looked at the poster photo again, shaking his head, "Ah, you were so young then." He looked at her, "And now, look at you so grown up, but not so much."

"Oh, no?"

"No, you will always be my little girl, my best miracle."

Esperanza took a bite of her pancakes and smiled, this was their special time together. Oscar's smile dropped away as he sipped his coffee, his eyes glancing out to the other diners in the room. "Now, listen to me, I have some things to tell you, something from my heart that must remain between you and me."

Esperanza slowed her eating, sipping her orange juice, watching Oscar's face very carefully,

"I want you to promise me you won't let anything stop you from graduating. No injuries, no disappointing grades, no boys, especially no boys. There will be time for them later. You becoming your best self is most important." He stopped to cut his ham and fried eggs, working the knife and fork deftly, "You know, when you were in your mother, I prayed you'd be a boy."

"Really?" Esperanza's surprise revealed the food on her tongue as her eyes expanded.

Oscar nodded, "It's true, I did. But when I saw you in the hospital, held you right there," He looked to his left forearm, his famous smile beaming again, "You were so tiny." He looked at her and kept smiling, "Well, then."

They laughed a moment together before Oscar resumed, "Your sister's like your mother. Don't misunderstand, that's not a bad thing, Esmeralda is passionate about everything she holds dear, she's a lioness, and she will do anything, *anything*, for her family. And like a lioness, she will kill without regret anyone that threatens anything she loves. But she's not a dreamer like you." Another bite of ham and eggs went to his mouth and he looked out to the dining room again.

"You are different, deeper than Esmeralda. Don't get me wrong, your sister is just as special to me, she's brought my grandsons into this world, and for that, I'm grateful. But you hold something special inside and," he shook his head, "I'm not sure what it is but, I'm certain that if you do not follow your heart, you will live a life worse than any of us can imagine." A bite of toast with jelly and swig of black coffee came and went. Oscar paused as his eyes looked past Esperanza, past restaurant glass doors, past the moment. "You have always been a dreamer. Dreams are wonderful, provided you understand their delicate nature. My father dreamed of me going to college, so, I went, but didn't know why or what to do? It was his dream, mine was still waiting for me to discover it. In this world, everyone *goes* to college, those who respect their dreams *finish* college: they graduate. Once you graduate, you have a certificate telling the world you're a serious person, someone who understands how knowledge and work weave together to produce results. If you want your dreams to happen, you have to build them, and work hard so that you see them someday, they won't just fall on you. If you fall in love, fall in love with someone willing to build their dreams with yours. Promise me, no matter what bad things may try to keep you from who you're meant to be, you will not let them take your dreams. Can you do that for me?"

Esperanza sat with eyes lined by soft tears of love and gratitude, nodding obediently. It's not often a child hears their parent grant permission to make mistakes or temporarily fail in pursuit of a greater, more satisfying life. Her heart seized the moment, cherishing it, taking it deep into her soul. Then, the magical smile, slightly lower in volume, emerged, sealing the moment's pure joy. Esperanza kept that moment deep within her, moving her through the days and months thereafter.

"Oh good, you two are cleaning," Yesenia observed as she stepped out from the kitchen, "I wondered why it was quiet?" She walked to the beverage machine and pressed her larger plastic cup against the ice dispenser. A few cubes dropped out, and then a grinding sound offered nothing more. "Marcos, we need ice cubes!" Yesenia called over her shoulder.

"You're going to need that new machine before he goes back to school, Mama," Ezzy said, wiping her cheeks. "Are you crying?" Yesenia walked to Ezzy, "What's wrong? Why're you crying?"

"I'm tired, Mama," Ezzy sniffed, "I didn't sleep well last night."

"Ooh, Baby," she lightly caressed Ezzy's hair, "Were you thinking of Arturo? I know, some nights I get lonely for your father." Yesenia fluttered her eyelashes as she wiped the corner of one eye. Esmeralda rolled her eyes to see Esperanza and sniffed, "Yeah Mama, that's it."

One glass door swung open and the bells hanging above it jingled, ringing the moment back to business. Carl walked in three steps before stopping to look at the women. As his eyes looked left to right and back again, he waited for acknowledgment from any one of them.

"Hello, Carl," Yesenia smiled broadly, "What can we do for you today?"

"Hello, could I speak with Esperanza, please?"

Yesenia stopped, uncertain how to answer, she smiled as her eyes drifted to her younger daughter replying, "But of course."

"A, hmm," as the room quieted, Carl cleared his throat before looking first to Ezzy, then Yesenia, then Espey. "I'm working tomorrow, but only until the afternoon. I wanted to ask if you'd like to go to dinner with me tomorrow night? Maybe go to a movie after, that is, once you're done here of course."

Now the room became uncomfortably small for Esperanza as her mother and sister turned their eagle-eyed focus directly on her. Espey glanced to the women watching, waiting for her answer more earnestly than Carl. She felt uneasy, like the room was slowly revolving around her, the air warmer, her vision narrowing on Carl's face.

"I'll be working until eight," Espey stammered.

"No, no, she'll be done by seven," Yesenia asserted, "we'll be closing at seven tomorrow night." Ezzy's face twisted as she squinted at Yesenia, "On Saturday?"

"I have been thinking of closing earlier on Saturday. We'll start tomorrow night." Ezzy looked directly at Espey, her mouth open in a perfect 'oh' as she brought her fingers to her cheek. Espey started to laugh but caught herself and looked to Carl, "Sure, Okay, I'll be here until seven."

"No, you go home at six and get ready, then come back here." Yesenia was now planning the entire date, "He can pick you up here." She turned to Carl, "Do you know where we live?"

"I can find it, Ma'am."

"Good. You won't be out too late, will you? My mother-in-law and I are light sleepers. We'll know when she gets home." Folding her arms across her chest, Yesenia raised one eyebrow.

"No Ma'am, not too late at all." Carl smiled.

"And you have honorable intentions, I mean, because her father is looking down on us, you know, he expects only the best for our daughter." Yesenia walked to Carl, looking up into those blue eyes she softly spoke, "*Dios mio eres hermosa.*"

"*Muchas gracias, Señora*," Carl smiled.

Instantly the three women gasped and brought their hands up to cover their mouths, their eyes wide as dinner plates, shining with surprise. Seeing he'd impressed everyone, Carl looked to Esperanza, "I'll meet you here, tomorrow night at seven."

He turned and walked out the door as the three women waited, squealing like excited school girls once the door closed.

******

Throughout the day, Esperanza was nervous, she hadn't been on a date in over three years. The thought of going that long without doing anything away from her mother and sister annoyed her. She talked to herself while preparing the counter for Saturday's business. "Three years? Really?" She asked while unpacking tortillas to stack in the warming oven. "Why?"

It wasn't a question to be answered for she knew instantly, no one of interest had been asking. "And why not?" she asked. Remembering a playground taunt that still stung as she cut tomatoes to make pico de gallo, she answered herself, "I'll tell you why not, there's no one here that is tall or brave or smart enough to be interested in me. I'm Esperanza, *mula gigante*." Making a grim face, she shredded heads of lettuce into the large stainless container. Esmeralda came from the kitchen, "Who you talking to?

Wiping her brow with the back of her hand, Espey replied, "Nobody, just myself."

"What about? You sound mad."

Espey pulled the rice pot to the counter, tilting it toward the empty bin in the steam well. "I'm not mad."

"Sounds like it to me."

"What am I doing? Going to a movie with this guy? Dinner too?"

"Why not?" Ezzy wiped her hands with a towel, then grabbed plastic forks and knives to put in their containers. "You need to get out, and have some fun." Next, Ezzy pulled a package of napkins out from under the condiment station, "If a man that good-looking asked me," her eyes wide, she smiled to her younger sister, "I might be gone for a weekend too!"

"You can do that. You're Esmeralda, the brave girl who's never afraid, always beautiful."

Ezzy stopped moving. She looked to Esperanza, her eyes slightly squinting, "I'm not that girl anymore. You're thinking like high school, long ago when we had no worries," she looked back to the parking lot, "or fears."

Espey watched Esmeralda leave the restaurant for a moment, searching again for the time when life seemed ready for the taking. "You know they still have that picture of you in Willoughby's, the one with you shooting." Esmeralda's look softened, "Papa used to ask to sit in the booth under it, he couldn't stop smiling, even when he ate. People would stop by and congratulate Mama and Papa. Everyone would talk about you, playing basketball, the men talking like you were their daughter. Shaking Papa's hand like you were someone famous. I wondered what it felt like, being famous."

Holding a container of guacamole to place in the ice well, Espey replied, "I just wanted to get away."

"Get away? How? On the court night after night? The whole town watching you play? Did you think a five-foot eleven-inch girl would be invisible? Newspapers, TV, they all came to see you. I could never do that, no matter how hard I tried." Ezzy looked to her sister with some envy but more pride, "I hoped you would fail but you never did, you kept winning, kept scoring, getting letters and visits. I went on dates, but you went out to the world."

Esperanza thought for a moment, remembering games she played in Utah, Wyoming and throughout the West. Staying in hotels for one or two nights, training table meals, and new shoes whenever requested, it felt like a distant dream now. She remembered being exhausted in some classes, traveling all night before to get back to campus. She thought to herself, *'I would love to be that sleepy again.'*

Esmeralda walked to the counter, directly opposite Esperanza. She put both her hands on top of the glass partition, "Look, I don't know about this Carl, but I'll tell you this, if you stay here a minute longer than you have to, you'll regret it every day. You got a college degree girl, go somewhere, make it work for you."

Ezzy's conviction resonated into Esperanza: pressing her lips together, she nodded obediently.

******

Saturday's business was lighter than usual, so Yesenia told the girls to start cleaning up at five o'clock. "Esperanza, you clear the counter, then take my car and go get ready."

"Mama, he's coming here at seven, why should I get ready so early?"

Landing both hands on her hips, Yesenia sternly replied, "That boy's going to be here at 6:30, you watch."

Espey looked to Ezzy, "Why would he come here at 6:30?"

Ezzy gave her a tilted head, pursed lips frown, "Really Espey? Have you seen the way he looks at you?" Yesenia agreed, "Uh-huh, he's been wanting to get you away for a long time, he's coming early, you'll see."

Esperanza continued working, cleaning and storing things in the walk-in refrigerator, trying not to think of how the evening would unfold. Showering at home, she waited to dry off completely before dressing. Esperanza carefully applied her mascara, eye-shadow and lipstick. She'd washed her jet-black hair, letting it air dry in the carport before making a double braid woven around her hairline to keep her cool. She chose a simple, full-skirted linen peasant dress, with bright traditional Mexican designs. Seeing herself in the full-sized mirror in her mother's bedroom, she remembered her father's proud words, *'Esmeralda's like her mother, a Mexican spitfire. Esperanza is like my mother, a Mayan queen.'*

No matter how hard she tried, Esperanza couldn't find anything else to delay her return. Not going the speed limit, slowing for yellow lights, taking the longest route back, nothing slowed her route, she arrived at the restaurant at 6:15 P.M. She noticed the silver Mercedes in its customary spot, but no other cars were in the parking lot. Taking the Cadillac around to the back door of the kitchen, she turned its engine off then dabbed her forehead and cheeks with a tissue, this air-conditioning problem needed to be fixed.

Opening the kitchen door, Espey saw Marcos struggling forward with a bulky trash bag. Holding the door for him, she waited outside as he proceeded to the dumpster. As he returned, she followed him into the kitchen, noticeably cooler than the outside. Marcos smiled, wiping his glistening forehead, "Thanks Tia." Esperanza smiled back at him, "You're welcome my good man."

Yesenia vigorously scrubbed the grill with her cleaning stone, quick back-and-forth strokes taking charcoal residue off the grate. Looking up, her face quickly shone as her eyes brightened, "OH, look at you!" she heralded, "You look so beautiful!"

Stopping to lean toward the dining room, Yesenia called out, "Ezzy! Come here! Quickly!"

A moment later, Ezzy rushed into the kitchen, "What? What is it?" Then she saw Esperanza standing by the walk-in refrigerator door, "OOhhh!! Look at you! Nenita! You're beautiful! Isn't she Mama? Doesn't she look beautiful?"

Yesenia stopped her labor to bask in her youngest daughter's aura, a young, beautiful, strong woman radiating with a purity and pride long-descendant from her ancestors. As the women reveled in their shared excitement, the bells over the door chimed. Yesenia queried, "Ezzy! I thought you locked the door?"

"Mama! How's he gonna get in if the doors' locked?"

In unison, they all stepped softly toward the dining room portal. Standing at the counter was a tall man wearing a light blue gingham checked shirt and blue jeans. As he looked to the parking lot, a full, cream-colored, cowboy hat titled back, keeping his hair and face obscured from view. His fingers thrust deep into the front pockets, his boots were black snakeskin, stirrup heels and pointed toes. He turned to their full view, it was Carl and it was 6:30 P.M. exactly.

"Oh my God," Yesenia whispered softly, "He's more gorgeous than I thought." Ezzy covered her mouth to muffle her laughter as Espey snapped, "Mama!"

Esperanza stepped out to the counter, blushing in surprise, "You're early."

Like a six-year-old on Christmas Eve, his eyes flashed nervously, "Uh-huh, I couldn't wait until seven." He licked his lips, hanging his thumbs inside each front pocket, waiting a moment before offering, "If we leave now, we can eat and then go to the movies."

"Oh, and what movie?" Esperanza smiled, letting her eyes flash, their lids fluttering ever so softly. Now Carl looked to Yesenia and Esmeralda, pausing to think about his answer. Looking back to Espey, "Well, this may sound dumb but, I like movies that are funny, you know?" He looked to the other women again, "I see enough cops and robbers every day, I want to laugh, forget about life for a while."

Nodding in agreement, Esmeralda smiled with Carl. Yesenia stood looking, unable to understand the romance of laughing in a theater. Carl returned his eyes to Esperanza, "There's this movie about animals trying to win a talent show, you know it?"

"Yes," Esperanza smiled, "My nephews went to see it."

"The cartoon? You're taking her to a cartoon movie?" Yesenia's one eyebrow rose in a perfect arch as she placed both hands on her hips, "What kind of *estúpida* takes a woman to a cartoon movie?" Turning to her mother with a direct stare, Esperanza objected, "Mama, it's fine."

Yesenia looked at her daughter, measuring the moment before surrendering, putting up both hands and stepping back. Espey looked back to Carl, "Let me get my purse and I'll be right out." Smiling broadly, Carl nodded and watched Ezzy, careful to avoid eye-contact with Yesenia.

Carl took Esperanza across town to a sports bar, explaining, "I figure the last thing you want to eat is Mexican food. It would either be boring or worse than your mother's cooking, and then you'd think I didn't have any imagination."

Once seated, they chatted about simple things like the weather, the cost of living, the price of gas, and almost anything that didn't reveal true feelings or perceptions. Each surprised the other with their entrée, Carl ordered the All-American burger and fries, which Esperanza found charming. Esperanza equally surprised Carl when she ordered the Tuscany Chicken breast on pasta with creamed spinach.

"Wow, I would've never thought you'd order something like that." He espoused, "Where'd you learn to like that?"

"College, in Colorado."

"Oh yeah? Which one?" Carl sipped from his water glass.

"UC, in Boulder."

"Did you graduate?"

"Yes, I did, my degree's in early education." Esperanza thought for a minute, trying to recall the last time she spoke of her degree in conversation: she couldn't remember. "How about you?" she asked Carl, "You go to college?"

A waiter brought a basket of rolls in one hand, and a small plate with butter tabs in the other. Laying them on the table, he quickly turned and walked away. Instantly, Carl opened the cloth napkin hiding the rolls before lifting the basket and extending it toward Esperanza, "Want one?"

"Uhm, sure." She reached for the roll, then took her knife and lifted a single slab of butter. "Did you graduate from college?" Esperanza's voice lilted through the question. Carl placed a bun on the small plate before him, then also lifting a tab of butter, he stopped his knife in mid-motion, turning his head to look toward the other tables, "Uhm, lemme think, did I graduate from college?"

Stopping to hear the answer, her mouth slightly open, Espey held the bun half bearing some butter about three inches from her face. A two, then three-second silence hung between them. Carl looked back to see her pose and his smile betrayed him as he snickered, "You gonna eat that or just hold it?"

Realizing how foolish she must appear, Esperanza looked at the bun before laughing at herself, "Well, are you going to tell me?"

Laughing a moment, Carl caught himself before admitting, "Yes, in Economics and Criminal Justice."

"Two? You have two degrees?" Esperanza blurted, "What are you doing here? Doing, … you know,"

"Border Patrol?" He set his bun down and looked around the room to see if anyone was watching them. Confident her remark had gone unnoticed, Carl explained, "It was the only job available in this region, down here.'

Espey thought for a moment, then she looked to him quizzically, "Wait, you wanted to come to Yuma?" He nodded, "I wanted to be somewhere near Mexico."

"Why? What would a man want here?"

Carl paused, letting his mind organize, rubbing his index fingers in small circles on the tablecloth. Then he began speaking slowly, his voice low, his eyes down, "I had a dream one night of meeting a woman someplace close to Mexico. I didn't know what town or state, but I knew it was really close to the border. Border Patrol and Customs representatives came to my campus trying to recruit new agents. One bonus of being accepted and hired, I got some of my student loans reduced. I've paid them off, and I've got two more years left before I can resign and go do what I really want to do."

Fully enthralled, Esperanza asked, "What's that?"

"Get a teaching certificate, teach econ, maybe at the high school level. Marry the woman of my dreams, have kids, take em' to cartoon movies." He looked to her face, glowing in his truthfulness, his willingness to speak openly, easily from his heart.

"You want to do that? Take your kids to cartoon movies?" She asked innocently. Looking directly into her eyes, Carl leaned forward on the table, opening his hands, palms facing inward, "Esperanza, I want to take *our* children to the movies."

Hearing those words, Esperanza froze, "What is it with you, men? You talk about babies, like you would really do anything beyond making one. Is that all you think about?"

Carl held his ground, "I'm not talking about right here, right now. I don't think you understand, but when I walked into La Cocina Colibri, the moment I saw you, I knew you were the woman of my dreams. I felt it, the hair on the back of my neck stood up. I wasn't looking for you, you came to me. I decided to wait until I could get you away from all the distractions of the restaurant. So I could tell you face to face. I've been waiting for you to see me."

"And tonight, you want to make a baby with me." She sat back in her chair, folding her arms over her chest. Carl too sat back, keeping his arms extended on the table while slowly shaking his head, "No, I want to make a life with you. I want a lot more than sex with you. My dream is to live each day with you, being in love with you. I've seen what that's like, that's what I want."

At that moment, the server arrived with their meals, laying down hers first, then his. Simultaneously, they both made the sign of the cross before looking at each other, breathing slowly, eye-to-eye, the moment holding them.

The movie made them both laugh out loud several times. Esperanza felt a little silly sitting in a theater on a Saturday night, watching animated creatures, laughing with this tall, handsome man who claimed she was the woman of his dreams. Watching Carl laugh in the movie screen's shadowy glare, she saw a softness in his profile reminiscent of her father. He respected her every move, opening the car door for her, letting her select their theater seats, and buying her any candy to eat during the movie. Slowly, over one-hundred-ten minutes of animated comedy, Esperanza began seeing Carl beyond his green federal uniform, the white pickup truck and holstered pistol. Here was a man who had a dream, a man who could make his way in the world, and in life. He was different from so many who had tried in various clumsy, immature ways to gain her attention. Certainly, a woman wants to be pursued but, she never wants to be trapped.

They left the theater and as they walked to the parking lot, he took her hand in his. She didn't resist, his hand was large and strangely comforting in the warm night air. Looking to the stars Carl said, "It's almost ten o'clock, I guess I should take you home."

They walked to the passenger side door, where he unlocked it and pulled the door handle, opening it fully. Esperanza turned to Carl and, looking up to him said, "Don't. Don't take me home yet."

"Where do you want to go?" He asked softly. Feeling she was lifting off the ground, Esperanza replied, "Wherever you are."

******

Tuesday morning, Espey pulled the carport kitchen door open ever so slowly, hoping to not make any sound. It didn't matter though, it was 7:30 A.M. and Marcos and Arturo Jr. sat at the kitchen table eating cereal from bowls, holding their heads with one hand, crunching and chewing and trying to wake up. Abuela Carlotta's slippered feet patted across the kitchen floor while she wiped the counter, moving dishes, humming an old song from Mexico. Neither boy reacted to her, nor did they notice Espey passing behind them.

Tip-toeing into the living room and then down the hallway, Espey carefully eyed her mother's bedroom door. It was closed, a sure sign Yesenia was sleeping. As Espey entered her bedroom, Ezzy came out of the bathroom, swiping the wall switch.

"Where you been?" Ezzy whispered, her words snapping crisply in the morning quiet. Espey stood in their bedroom saying nothing, quickly looking to her sister, bringing an extended index finger up, over her pursed lips, "Ssshhhh!" She waved her free hand, beckoning Ezzy toward her, "C'mere!"

Looking at the closed bedroom door, Ezzy stepped quickly, lightly on the tile, bringing her knees almost waist high, rushing into the bedroom before Espey closed the door behind her. Once the handle snapped shut, Espey went to her bed and sat, drawing her knees up to her chin. Ezzy curiously watched her sister. Only the smile on Espey's face was brighter than the morning sun. Her cheeks were luminous, her eyes sparkled, and she felt lighter than air. Ezzy sat on her bed and let her disapproval melt in the glow of her sister's happiness, "You slept with him, didn't you."

Espey nodded quickly, her smile impish, as though admitting to eating the last cookies. Ezzy nodded twice, weaving her fingers together, "And now you're in love, eh?" Ezzy sat still watching her sister, then added, "And you told him you loved him, right?"

Espey remained still, the smile not fading or changing before she said, "No, he said he loved me." Ezzy feared the worst of heartaches coming for her sister, "Of course, he did, what did he say when he was finished with you?"

"He asked when I could get off from work? He wants to take me home to his parents in Illinois, he wants us to get married. Not in Illinois, but soon." Espey covered her mouth with her fingers, watching Ezzy process the words one by one. After some thinking, Ezzy side-eyed Esperanza, "If he wants to marry you, where's the ring? Did you pick one out?"

Now confident her sister would help, Espey relaxed, "I told him my ring size, told him I wanted white gold and a big diamond like white girls get." She looked at the ring finger on her left hand, "He's going to Phoenix today to get something and he'll bring it to me Thursday night before we close."

Ezzy relaxed, then looked to the door, "Don't get too happy, she's been in a bad mood." Espey looked to their closed door, "Why, what happened?"

"I don't know. She came home Sunday and been a beast all weekend."

"Don Esteban?"

Shrugging her shoulders, Ezzy looked to the window, "Ignacio brought her here about one o'clock. He didn't say anything. She came in, slammed the door, and went to her room." Ezzy looked back to Espey, "She yelled at the boys for playing too loud in the backyard. Abuela brings her some food and drinks every now and then, but she don't say nothing. I don't know."

"You think they split up?" Espey asked, her mind finding the thought incredulous.

"I hope not. Can you imagine work if they did?"

"You think Don Esteban would still come to the back?" Espey naively asked.

"Espey! He owns the restaurant!" Ezzy whispered sharply.

"He does?"

"Yyeeaahh! How do you think Mama affords her clothes and shoes and stuff? She can barely pay us and the bills. He uses the restaurant to run his money and keep it away from the IRS. We better hope he hasn't got a new *novia*. If he does, we're done."

Their conversation was interrupted by the front doorbell ringing. The sisters looked to each other wondering who could be at the front door before eight o'clock in the morning? Next came the sounds of footsteps down the tiled hall, followed by a knock and Marco's voice, "Abuela, Ignacio is at the door."

Ezzy and Espey jumped off their beds and opened the door to see Yesenia coming out of her room, her hair wild, eyes puffy, blackened by ruined mascara, cheeks swollen. She looked to her daughters, first Esmeralda then Esperanza, whom she eyed warily, warning in a raspy voice, "I'll deal with you later."

Yesenia went to the living room door where Ignacio patiently waited. They spoke in quick, hushed phrases of Spanish. As Ignacio nodded and smiled, Yesenia's knees slightly buckled. Making the sign of the cross, she proclaimed "*Madre de dios*!"

Turning quickly, she saw her family all standing, watching, wondering. She looked back to Ignacio, "Wait for me in the car." He nodded and went outside. Yesenia turned and with her head down, walked between her daughters, back down the hall and into her bedroom. Before closing the door, she called back to everyone, "We still have a business to run! Get to work on time!" The door closed loudly and everyone returned to their usual start of the week: showers, dressing, leaving at 9:45 and driving across Yuma in the hot, bright morning.

Marcos, Esperanza and Esmeralda opened the restaurant kitchen door and went about preparing to meet Tuesday's demands. At 10:45

A.M., the silver Mercedes pulled up to the same door and let Yesenia out. She entered quickly, not acknowledging anyone. In the bathroom, she changed out of her clothes into her shorts, tank top and running shoes. Pulling on her apron as she walked to the kitchen, she made no eye contact, curtly commanding, "Esperanza, come with me."

Espey looked to Ezzy who quickly made the sign of the cross as she watched her sister dutifully walk to the kitchen. Stopping two feet from her mother, Espey asked, "Yes, Mama?"

"Where were you all weekend?" Yesenia picked up the large stone brick to scrub the grill. She still hadn't made eye contact when she asked, "Marcos, did you check the garbage cans? Are they empty?"

"Yes, Abuela," He responded obediently.

Espey waited, watching her mother attack the grill, the crunching, rasping sound of the block sliding back and forth on the metal. Yesenia called out again, "Esmeralda!?" From the counter area the response came back, "Yes, Mama?"

"Do you have enough cash in the drawer?"

"Yes, Mama," Ezzy called back, "I got the usual amount from the bank on the way here." Waiting patiently, Espey looked to the front counter area briefly before looking at Yesenia who went to the walk-in refrigerator.

"Esmeralda! Do we have deliveries today? Meat? Lettuce? Tomatoes?" Having seen a Yesenia tantrum before, Ezzy gave another polite answer from the dining room, "Yes, Mama, I got it handled."

Watching closely, Espey stood still as Yesenia, Marcos and Ezzy all kept moving, preparing everything needed for the lunch rush. After minutes of silence, Espey turned to go back to the counter. Yesenia barked, "I didn't say you could leave!"

"Mama, this is ridiculous."

"Don't you talk to me like that little girl. You show me respect, I'm still your mother!"

"Mama, I know that."

"You think you can just take off, go around with this *burra*, like some cheap *puta*?"

"Mama, stop! He's not like that!" Esperanza retorted.

"Don't raise your voice to me!" Yesenia charged, lifting her chin to look down her nose, albeit up into Esperanza's neck and chest area.

"DON'T YOU TALK TO ME LIKE THAT!" Esperanza's voice filled the restaurant, "I'm not some whore you can insult! I'm a grown woman, too! And you will not talk to me like I'm a child." Espey's eyes were red, anger shaking her chin and torso. Yesenia stood still, eyeing her daughter's clenched right fist. Truly surprised to see her child acting so strong, so independent.

"Oh, I see," Yesenia smiled, "Now, you're going to tell me you're a grown-up, how you know everything." Yesenia took a step forward, "You think you're better than me, college girl? Is that it? You think you know more than me, eh? All that college and look at you, you're just like me and your sister! Working like us, cooking, cleaning, and hoping to get away someday. But you're going nowhere." Looking out the dining room windows, beyond the parking lot images undulating in the rising heat, the older woman sighed.

"When are you going to learn, there's nothing any of us can do. These men keep chasing us, lying to us, giving us babies to raise, so they too can be killed or disappear."

"I'm not like you Mama, I can go and have a life. Carl wants a life with me. He loves me." Esperanza wistfully remembered her weekend, the laughing, soft touches, the nights of passion. "And I want my life with him."

"Oh my god, you gave yourself to him, didn't you?" Yesenia leaned on the grill edge with one hand, "*Bebita*, a man will tell you anything to get between your legs. Once you give in, you've got nothing left to offer."

"No, Mama, it's not like that." Esperanza felt tears forming against her mother's cynicism, "He knows where he's going in life. He wants his dream with me."

Again, Yesenia's indignance rose between them, "Oh, you've got a man who's going somewhere? Well, your man tried to have my man killed so, I wouldn't be so sure young lady. My Esteban doesn't take attempts on his life lightly. Your man should leave now if he knows what's good for him."

"What are you talking about?" Esperanza asked.

"Don't play innocent with me." Yesenia took a large skillet down from the rack, placing it on the stove, "Men came at my Esteban, early Sunday morning but, thanks be to GOD, they couldn't kill him." Yesenia tilted her head to one side, her snarl and side-eye look staring at Esperanza, "He's at Regional Center, his men will get everyone, including *your* man."

Fear seized Esmeralda, and her stomach began churning. Searching her heart, she knew Carl wasn't capable of such duplicity. "Mama, you're wrong. Carl wouldn't do something like that. He's an honorable man."

"Oh! He's honorable, huh? What do you know, foolish girl."

Esperanza's heart refused to yield to Yesenia's threats. Yes, she was her daughter, but she was also a grown woman. A woman capable of making her own decisions. Capable of finding life somewhere beyond all she had known, somewhere new where her life could be enjoyed. A life of love and happiness, not fear and sorrow. "I love him and I know he loves me. You'll see, he's buying me a ring, he wants to marry me. He wants to take me away somewhere where women are wives and not widows."

Espey's words stung Yesenia, bringing to mind Oscar, Ezzy's pain from losing Arturo, and the constant fears and sorrows of three women's and two boy's vulnerable lives. The weight of reality pushed Yesenia's shoulders and torso down, wobbling her as her tears flowed off her cheeks onto the hot skillet's chopped meat. She cried into the steaming food, "I wanted to be a dancer. I was seventeen when I saw him. What did I know? He said he loved me and would never leave me. What did I know?"

Waving her hand, she sent Esperanza back to the counter. The rest of the day, Yesenia would intermittently cry or grunt, handling skillets, pots and pans roughly, saying nothing, smothered by her emotions. Walking to her side of the counter, Espey looked at Esmeralda standing dutifully at the cash register, single tear streams sliding down each cheek, sniffling softly, trying to keep her emotions in check as the first patrons entered.

Espey felt her tears building, a combination of fear and frustration. Feeling her words were meaningless and would disappear into time going forward, a day, a week, a year. One after another the days and months could melt away, and five years from now, she'd still be standing at this counter, older but no closer to her dream. She had to strike out now. Carl offered a chance for a new, different life that could be enjoyed, not just survived.

Wednesday followed Tuesday's work without laughter, fun, or sisterhood in the restaurant. Everyone except Marcos was tense, snappish, whispering, and politely responding but never making eye contact. Avoidance was preferred to disagreement, misunderstanding, despair. The self-inflicted isolation became more comfortable with each day's passing, hardening each woman's belief that only she truly understood their shared circumstance.

******

Thursday started like any other weekday, opening the restaurant, preparing the counter, the kitchen coming to life through sizzling and savory aromas. The lunch crowd was lighter than usual, giving Espey and Ezzy time to fully sweep the dining room and patio. Marcos was dispatched to empty the waste containers while Yesenia checked the walk-in refrigerator and made a list of foodstuffs to order. Wiping down all the tables inside and out, Espey looked out to see the silver Mercedes roll into the parking lot. It went directly to the back door, to Don Esteban's roost. Walking back into the kitchen, Ezzy followed Espey and heard their mother's squeal as she ran to Don Esteban. Stopping before him, she wrapped her arms around his neck as he steadied himself with a cane in one hand. His other arm went around her waist as he kissed her cheek.

"*Mi amor*!" Yesenia proclaimed, swaying her lover's body slightly left and then right. "I knew you'd come back to me! Thank God! Let me look at you!" She released his neck and stepped backward, scanning the man's body up and down, her hands holding her cheeks as she gushed, "You're so handsome! You look wonderful!"

Only when Yesenia separated from Don Esteban could Espey and Ezzy see the large bandage around Esteban's left leg. He wore a slipper-type shoe, having a flat, solid sole, keeping his ankle fixed by an elastic brace. At mid-calf, a winding bandage of gauze and elastic almost four inches wide, covered a wound.

"What happened to him?" Espey whispered. "I don't know," Ezzy replied, "but I'll bet that's a gunshot."

"You think?"

"Yep." Ezzy looked back to the front windows to see a familiar white pickup truck roll in and park. "And now, it looks like you got company."

Esperanza stepped back out to the counter and watched Carl Ralston walk across the parking lot toward the restaurant's front glass doors. Espey's eyes focused on his right hand holding something small. Carl looked to Don Esteban's Mercedes near the back patio door. He nodded and kept walking to the glass doors. Pulling one open, he smiled broadly upon seeing Esperanza waiting behind the counter. Esmeralda came from the kitchen and seeing Carl, she became nervous. Carl walked right to the counter, his smile growing with each step. Esperanza smiled too, stepping into the open space between the cash register and beverage machine.

"Hi," he smiled, "I came to see you."

"Hi" she smiled back, "What about?"

Stopping two feet before her, Carl bent down on one knee, his right hand lifting the small, dark blue box with gold trim up in its palm.

"MAMA!" Ezzy yelled, "MAMA COME OUT HERE!"

Carl and Espey's heads turned to Ezzy, eyes wide with surprise. Hearing no reply, Ezzy called again, "MAMA, COME QUICKLY!"

"What is it, Niñeta? What!?" Yesenia called back, her voice getting louder as she came out of the kitchen. Seeing Carl before Esperanza on one knee, the small box presented, she gasped, "*Madre de Dios*! What is this?"

Slightly hobbling on his cane, Don Esteban came from the kitchen and took in the sight. Esmeralda and Yesenia stood silent, their mouths and eyes wide with surprise. Carl knelt holding the blue box open, a shining white gold ring and large diamond gleaming brilliantly against navy-blue velour padding.

As the moment's disbelief silenced everyone, Carl spoke, "Esperanza Mejia, ever since I saw you, I've dreamed of how my life could be as your husband. I know I could live without you, but it really wouldn't be living. I will do everything in my power to keep you happy and certain of my love. All I ask is that you marry me. Will you have me as your husband? Will you make me the happiest man on earth, Please?"

Tears burst from Esperanza's eyes as she brought both hands up to cover her mouth, nodding vigorously, she cried, "Yes, yes, yes!"

With that, Carl stood up and reached for Esperanza as she extended her arms and stepped into his. Esmeralda then stepped to them, wrapping her arms around both her sister and her soon-to-be-brother-in-law. The three wavered slightly as happiness saturated them all down to their bones.

"I'm seeing two miracles today!" Yesenia proclaimed as she turned to Esteban to hug him once again. Stepping to him, she opened her arms and said to Marcos standing nearby, "Nièto, come here, today, we are happy!" She and Esteban hugged the boy, and for a moment six people shared tears of happiness and jubilation: but only for a moment. Both glass doors swung open violently as five young men rushed into the dining room, "That's right bitches! Get on the fucking floor!"

All five wore light blue paisley bandanas, some in shorts, some in long, baggy black denim. Each one hiding under a white COVID N-95 face mask. The leader in front wore a familiar gold crucifix and blue scorpion tattoo on his forearm. Everyone recognized Joaquin's voice as he waved a chrome pistol and barked, "I said get on the floor!"

Carl turned, pulling Espey and Ezzy behind him with his free hand, the other closed the ring box and held it tightly. Don Esteban, too moved purposely to get Yesenia and Marcos out of sight, pushing them into the kitchen, toward the walk-in refrigerator. The other four invaders fanned out behind Joaquin, two of them openly displaying handguns, the others showing only empty hands.

"What do you want Joaquin!?" Ezzy called over Carl's shoulder.

One of Joaquin's men, Felipe, lifted his pistol and pointed it toward her, "Shut up bitch, we do the talking!" His gun hand trembled as he shuffled his feet slightly, looking around to his left and right.

Carl raised his left hand slowly, palm facing Joaquin, "Now, let's all calm down, okay? No reason for anyone to get hurt."

"Shut up!" Joaquin snapped. He looked to Carl's right hand, "What's in your hand? Show me!"

Watching Joaquin's eyes, Carl paused, never blinking, breathing slowly, calmly. Joaquin watched Carl just as closely, breathing quickly, the gun in his hand quivering. "Lemme see what 'choo got!" Joaquin demanded.

Taking a deep breath, Carl exhaled slowly and opened his palm, showing the small, dark blue box with gold trim. Carl looked at the box and then at Joaquin, his face becoming stern, resolute. Then, Don Esteban stepped forward, commanding, "Joaquin Avilar, what do you want? Why're you bothering these people?"

Trying to minimize his limp and use of the cane, the older man stepped forward, chin up, eyes fixed on the intruders. Joaquin looked away from Carl, instead pointing his pistol to Don Esteban, "You *anciano*, I came for you."

Stepping to his right, Joaquin eyed Don Esteban as he steadied his hand. "Lorenzo Martinez, my cousin, do you know him? He's in the hospital with a bullet in his brain. They say they can't operate or he could die." Joaquin's chin wobbled briefly, "They say he'll always be a vegetable."

Carl casually dropped his hand with the box down to his side, sliding it into his pants pocket while watching Joaquin and the other four staring at Don Esteban. Taking one more step forward, Don Esteban lowered his tone, "Joaquin, these people had nothing to do with you or me or Lorenzo. Come around to the back and let's discuss these unfortunate events."

Don Esteban smiled, extending his free hand at arm's length, then sweeping it back in the direction of the rear patio. Joaquin looked at the women, then Carl, then back to Don Esteban, "Oh no, old man, I see what you're up to, your man Ignacio, he's back there, waiting to kill us."

With the dialog between Joaquin and Don Esteban paused. Carl's right hand moved slowly to unsnap the holster guard over his pistol. Watching the five *'escorpiones'*, he saw them all intently watching Don Esteban, frozen by his presence. The air became heavy and still, time stopped as every person felt their heart beating underneath each breath. Joaquin then gave a devilish grin, "No, you will come with me. Tomorrow, they will pull the plug on Lorenzo, but you'll be dead by then."

Suddenly, the atmosphere exploded, slowing everything, 'BRACKA-BRACKA-BRACK!!' A sound like waves crashing on all ears followed, the sound of glass cascading to the tiled floor, 'SSSHHHHEEEEAAAASSSSHHHH!!'

The chests of the two boys closest to the front doors exploded, spraying flesh and bone and blood forward, they fell never knowing what hit them. Carl shoved Esperanza to the floor, under a table and chairs as he pulled his weapon and crouched down. As he fell down, Joaquin fired a shot that struck the beverage machine before he turned to the doors. Felipe and the last boy were too stunned to react. Pulling one door open, Ignacio fired again, 'BRACK-BRACK-BRACK,' striking Felipe in his left thigh.

Seeing Ignacio outside before he fired, Don Esteban turned just in time, pushing Yesenia and Marcos back into the kitchen, hobbling and then crouching at one edge of the doorway to watch. Turning again, Joaquin pointed to Carl and fired, striking him just behind the left ear. Carl returned fire, missing Joaquin before he collapsed on the floor. At that moment a blast came from the cash register as Esmeralda's sawed-off shotgun roared, BLA-BLACKK!! Opening Joaquin's abdomen, shearing off his tattooed forearm just below the elbow.

Terrified, Felipe tried firing his pistol at Ezzy, his shots striking the floor first, then the counter. Calmly, Ezzy broke the shotgun's breach, the two spent casings popping up, then falling to the floor. She reached under the counter, pulled out two fresh rounds and coolly loaded each barrel before snapping the breach closed and stepping forward. The last boy stood frozen, his pistol pointing down to the floor. Grabbing his right wrist with his left hand, the pistol shaking, Felipe attempted to steady his aim. Esmeralda calmly declared, "You motherfucker's killed my Arturo, didn't you?"

The shotgun level on her hip, with her left hand on the barrel stock, Ezzy pulled the triggers, first right, then the left. In the same instant, Ignacio fired again, 'BRACK-BRACK' his bullets striking Felipe's back as Ezzy's first blast struck his pistol hand and shredded the left hand over his wrist. The last boy took her second blast in the chest, his eyes never blinking, dying on the floor with them still open.

"CCAAARRLLL!!!" Esperanza screamed as she crawled across the floor to him. His body crumpled against the base of the counter, blood pulsating out behind his ear, flowing down his neck. She pulled herself to him, calling out, "MAMA! EZZY! CALL AN AMBULANCE! CALL THE POLICE!!"

Sitting up, she pulled her tee-shirt off and began wrapping it around Carl's head. "Carl! I'm here, it's gonna be okay, okay?" Her tears blurred her vision as she lifted his upper torso onto her lap, "Stay with me baby! I'm right here! Stay with me, please, Carl!"

"Ignacio, get the car!" Don Esteban yelled. Yesenia got up from covering Marcos and went to her purse. Pulling out her cellphone, she dialed 9-1-1, in an instant she started shrieking, "Yes, send an ambulance, right away! What? Oh, La Cocina Colibri, 486 Gila Street! HURRY! What? Yes, I'll stay here!

Ezzy ran back to the kitchen, "MARCOS! WHERE ARE YOU!?" From behind the refrigerator door, the boy whimpered, "I'm right here, Mama." With shotgun still in hand, Ezzy ran to her son, pulling him to her, wrapping her arms around him, asking, "Are you alright? Are you hurt?"

"No Mama, Abuela covered me on the floor." The boy started crying softly at first, trembling before exploding with howls as the night's terror began settling into his soul. From the dining room, Espey called out, "EZZY, where are you?!"

Holding her oldest son, her tears and gulps cascading over his hair, she called back, "I'm back here, you okay?"

"Carl's bleeding bad!" Espey called.

Ezzy looked into Marcos' eyes, "Stay here baby, I'll be right back." She kissed his forehead and went to the dining room. Laying the shotgun on the counter next to the register, she paused to take in the macabre scene. Joaquin's body lay ahead of Felipe's, their blood pooling over the tiles. The two boys by the doors, shot by Ignacio were lying on the floor close to a table. The last boy with a pistol, lay on the floor, his eyes open to the ceiling as the acrid vapors of gunpowder slowly swirled under the ceiling fans.

Stepping smoothly over the corpses, Ignacio walked to Don Esteban. Looking at the room's carnage he said, "We should go." Nodding his head, Don Esteban replied, "I'll meet you out back." He looked to Yesenia and nodded before tottering through the kitchen and out the back patio's wrought-iron door. The Mercedes sped off, heading away from town, out toward the foothills.

Cradling Carl in her lap, Esperanza spoke softly through her tears, "Carl, baby please stay here, please don't die." Closing her eyes, she pleaded, "Jesus, have mercy, please, please have mercy, keep him alive, please Jesus." The minutes dragged before the siren's wail grew louder as it neared the restaurant.

Clouds of dust quickly followed the ambulance and then two Yuma Metropolitan Police vehicles, delivering four officers who entered cautiously, unlike the three paramedics who ran to Esperanza's wails for help. As one paramedic looked into Carl's eyes with a small flashlight, another brought a large valise to the floor, opening it immediately and extracting multiple items of care. The third checked the five bodies, telling officers, "I'm not sure there's anything I can do here."

One officer stopped at the cash register and with latex gloved hand, lifted the shotgun, "Where'd this come from?" Yesenia stepped from the kitchen and looked to the officer, "It's mine. These *ladrones* tried to rob us. I had to defend my family."

The second paramedic asked the first, "How's he doing?"

"Gotta pulse, it's weak, we need to move. Get the cart, I'll start the IV, notify Regional we got a cerebral GSW – need immediate full surgical. Let's move!" The second para jumped up and as he passed, he tapped the third's shoulder, "Forget them, we got a live one."

******

The hospital intensive care unit was dark, cool and quiet. In Room 338, Carl Ralston lay tethered to wires and tubes, soft beeps and occasional clicks of technology all working to keep him alive. Over in the building's extension, two floors below, a neurologist, neurosurgeon and two radiologists all standing with arms folded over chests, some index fingers to lips, stared up to white-gray images on black sheets laying over florescent lights, murmuring, wondering.

"Remarkable," said the neurosurgeon. "I know," The neurologist replied, "His head leans one way and he's a mess on the floor. He leaned the other and now, here we are."

The lead radiologist scratched the back of his head, "Everything I see tells me the bullet ran an irregular path under the brain, behind the spinal column and over to just behind the right ear." He looked to the others, "It's the damnedest thing I've ever seen."

"Where is he now?" the second radiologist asked.

"Up in ICU, intubated and on a drip, right?" The neurosurgeon looked to the neurologist who nodded in affirmation. The lead radiologist looked to the neurosurgeon, "So, what're you thinking?"

The neurosurgeon looked to the neurologist, nodding in agreement. "I think we go in, get the bullet out, watch for any further hemorrhaging, wait a day or two and see if anything else happens."

******

After the paramedics took Carl away, two more squad cars brought four officers, and the investigation began. The women were interviewed collectively and individually. Ezzy made Yesenia get a top from the bathroom for Espey and finally, at ten o'clock they were released. Pulling away from the restaurant, Espey watched the yellow police tape being wrapped around the entire building.

"When will that come down?" she asked.

"What?" Ezzy answered.

"That yellow tape, you know, 'Crime Scene – Do Not Cross'."

Yesenia leaned on her left hand, her right controlling the steering wheel. Hot air rushed through the windows as the women silently relived horrific moments, trying to think of anything else. Staring out the windshield, Yesenia spoke, "Espey, be careful, that blouse cost me twenty-eight dollars."

Esperanza's eyes flashed left, annoyed by her mother's selfishness. After a moment, she shook her head and looked out to the passing streetlights. The twelve-minute drive in the hot night air was quiet. Marcos had fallen asleep and Ezzy rested her head on the rear seat top. Weighed down by the shock of life changing before their eyes, again, each person stumbled to their bedroom hoping to sleep and forget.

"I can't believe it," Ezzy muttered as she slipped her jeans off before removing her tee-shirt, letting both lie on the floor where they landed. "What happened tonight?" She plopped down on her bed, sitting and looking to Espey, "My son saw five people killed, right before his eyes. And I killed some of them. What's wrong with me?"

Taking a hangar and placing the blouse gently over it, Espey sighed heavily, "Over two thousand years ago, our ancestors came from Asia, walking south. They would stop, build villages, live and then move again." Unbuttoning her jeans, she pulled the zipper down and began removing one leg, "Twelve hundred years ago, the Anasazi came through here, going to Mexico and beyond. Some stopped, forming tribes, some kept going, all the way to Chile and Peru." The second leg came out of her jeans and she began folding them up to place on top of her dresser.

"The Maya settled in Yucatan, then the Aztecs made them slaves, killing them for religious sacrifices to their gods. Everywhere, tribes began killing other tribes, for gold, water or livestock or women." Espey exhaled heavily, "Then the Spanish came and they either killed or made slaves of everyone." Esperanza slowly laid down to her pillow on top of the sheets, putting one forearm over her forehead, "We've been doing it to ourselves for a thousand years."

"Where'd you hear that?"

"A class I took in college on Indigenous North American Cultures," Espey replied. "It's always been men killing each other, leaving women to survive." Taking her arm off her forehead, Espey looked to her sister through the darkness, "They came down here to make things better and they've been leaving us ever since."

Esmeralda turned and lay down on her bed, looking to the ceiling she folded her hands across her stomach, "Think it'll ever change?"

"You're the Mom, what do you think?"

******

Friday morning started quietly as only Abuela Carlotta and Arturo Jr. awoke before ten o'clock. Esperanza awakened and lay in her bed, the morning light coming in through the window above her. She looked to Esmeralda's back, her sister curled up facing the wall, her sheet stopping below her bare shoulders.

Hearing Yesenia come out of her bedroom, Espey waited, listening intently. Soft footsteps down the tiled hallway to the kitchen were followed by softer Spanish, greetings and pouring coffee. Reluctantly, Espey got up and found a pair of shorts to wear. Looking back to Ezzy's still form, the sounds of gunfire and falling bodies echoed in Espey's mind. She didn't see the pull of the shotgun triggers, but she did hear Ezzy sentence the boys to death. Despite admiring how fearless Ezzy could be, Esperanza knew she would now see her sister differently.

As Espey poured a cup of coffee, she heard Esmeralda's cellphone sounding. Three sets of recurring chime sounds rang from the bedroom before a raspy "Hello?" Rubbing her forehead, Espey listened, "Yeah, what?" then, "Really? When?" A pause followed, and Espey sipped the hot solution as she walked toward the hallway.

"How long?" Ezzy's voice was scratchy, so Espey turned back to the kitchen. "Then what?" came from behind Espey as she stepped quickly to the cupboard and opened its door. A creaking sound from the bed signaling Ezzy's standing was followed by footsteps into the bathroom, its door closing. Taking a drinking glass from the cupboard, Espey went to the five-gallon water bottle on its stand and filled the glass, Ezzy always liked a glass of cool water first thing in the morning.

Standing at the counter, Espey watched Arturo Jr. lift another spoonful of cereal to his mouth. Crunching softly, he stared blankly at the bowl. Abuela Carlotta pulled dishes from the drying rack and put them away while Yesenia sat opposite her grandson, staring out the sliding glass doors across the open backyard.

The bathroom door opened with the sound of a toilet flushing in the background. Ezzy walked back into her bedroom and after finding her tee-shirt, headed down the hall. Turning into the small kitchen, she first went to Arturo Jr. and, kissing his forehead, cooed, "Good morning precious boy." She then looked to her mother who kept staring far away. Seeing Abuela Carlotta she respectfully offered,

"Buenos dias, Abuela." The elderly lady nodded and softly replied, "Buenos dias."

As she looked at her younger sister, Ezzy spied the cool glass of water, slightly frosted by warm air's condensation. Reaching for it, she smiled to Espey, "Thank you." Taking a sip, then another, Ezzy looked Espey directly in the eye and jerked her head ever so slightly to the right, signaling, 'Let's go.' Espey watched the kitchen as she walked to the living room and hallway. Taking quick, light steps, the two sisters went to their bedroom and closed the door.

"He's alive" Ezzy whispered.

"He, … Carl?" Espey whispered back, bringing her hand to her mouth, trying to capture her question. Her eyes searched the small space between them as she processed the miracle. Looking to Ezzy, she asked, "How do you know?"

"Maria Alvarez, remember her? She just called. She's a nurse in intensive care. She says he's scheduled for surgery later today, they're gonna try to get the bullet out."

"Oh, oh my God," Espey's tears started forming as her body trembled. She placed her coffee cup down on her dresser, "I've gotta go there, I gotta be with him."

"Sshh, sshh," Ezzy softly touched her sister's forearm, "You can't, not yet." She stroked the forearm softly, gently. "They've got armed guards outside his room. Nobody can get in to see him except the doctors." Now Espey's tears began running down her cheeks, "But, I have to go!"

"Sshh, sshh" Ezzy repeated as she looked to the closed door, "Don't let her hear you." Ezzy put her glass down and embraced Espey, "Maria says after surgery, tonight maybe, you can get in there."

"How?"

"Her brother Jaime, he's a county sheriff remember? He's got guard duty tonight, outside Carl's room, starting at ten o'clock. He'll be the only one, he'll let you in, Maria will make sure."

"You sure?"

"Hey, Maria don't play. She tells her little brother to let you in, that's all it takes."

Realizing she would have to accept forces of life beyond her reach, Esperanza spent the day trying to relax, trying to avoid thinking of all the possible outcomes she didn't want to face. Yesenia took Espey with her to the restaurant to see the surreal remnants of their former life. Multiple tracks of police sedans and SUVs, a firetruck and two ambulances wound through and around the dirt parking lot in circles out to Gila Street. Bright yellow tape surrounded the building, flapping and twisting insincerely in the wind. The shattered glass doors showed black openings opposite dusty reflections still fixed in position.

Calling the police department, Yesenia nervously tapped her fingernails against the steering wheel while waiting for a human response. The hot wind blew through the Cadillac omnipotently, tossing their hair, flicking dust in their eyes. Finally, a voice prompted Yesenia's full attention, "Yes, hello, this is Yesenia Mejia, I was wondering if you could tell me when I can get back into my restaurant?"

The voice disappeared back into silence as Yesenia bit her lip, looking at the building, dust blowing across the patio tables. The voice returned, surprising her, 'Uh-huh, I'm here," she listened, "Three to four weeks! How come so long?" She pushed her sunglasses back up on her nose, "But I need to open Tuesday! I got to clean up, get the doors fixed, you know?" Her head turned to Espey who watched closely. "No, that's not right! I didn't do nothing! They came in and started shooting! Why should I suffer?!" Yesenia looked through the windshield, towards the expressway, cars and trucks whizzing by. "I understand there's an investigation, but I got bills to pay. I need to have my business open."

Espey wondered what happened to Don Esteban? She was holding Carl when the paramedics approached, focused on his head wrapped in the pink tee-shirt she'd worn, the crimson stain growing, blood covering her hand and arm.

"No! No! You can't do that! I need my business open. Please, I'm begging you, let me open, please?" A second passed before Yesenia jerked the cell phone from her ear, "Uugghh!! These people! They don't care about anyone." Her thumb jabbed at the keypad, ending the call before she tossed the phone into the center console, "This is all because of your boyfriend!" she charged Espey.

"My boyfriend!?" Esperanza gasped, "Your boyfriend was who they came for! Carl was proposing to me, remember?" Tears and emotions started overwhelming Esperanza's mind and heart, "My boyfriends' fighting for his life in the hospital, where's your boyfriend?"

"Don't you speak like that!" Yesenia snarled, her head quivering with each word. "You have no right!"

"I have no right!? Look at us! Your man did something and now we're both paying for it! I have no right? When did I give him power over my life?" Wiping her eyes, Espey looked out her window, "Two and half years ago, I came to help you. I work every day, helping you for almost nothing and look, what have we got? Again, we have to survive, by ourselves."

"Oohh, I forgot, you're the smart college girl, you know everything don't you?" Yesenia pulled down her sunglasses, "Well, if you're so smart, how come the only man ever interested in you got his ass shot when he had his own gun? What kind of idiot has a gun and doesn't know how to use it? Yesenia's smile grew, her eyes flashing devilishly. Esperanza calmly replied, "What kind of woman sleeps with a man who runs away?"

"You little bitch!" Yesenia shrieked, "Don't you talk to me like that!" And in one quick swipe, Yesenia's free hand slapped Esperanza's cheek, a loud skin-on-skin, cracking sound. Esperanza's head twisted sideways from the blow, her eye closing momentarily before she refocused directly on her mother, staring into the flashing eyes, "That all you got?"

"YYEEAAAUUGGHH!!" Yesenia screamed as she lunged across the console, her nails aimed at Esperanza's eyes. Esperanza reacted, bringing both her hands up to snare Yesenia's, stopping her mid-lunge, "MAMA! STOP!"

The two women swayed, neither having control, "You have always thought you're better than me!" Yesenia hissed, "You have no idea what I had to put up with. Your father couldn't keep me happy, he wanted to play basketball with you instead of taking me dancing. I was supposed to be a dancer, on stage in New York. He kept me here with his smile and good looks."

Yesenia sagged back into her seat, looking at the restaurant, her disappointment pulling her away. The mother and daughter sat in silence, each uncertain of their future, each resenting their present, captured and haunted by dreams and fairy-tale lives they held in their hearts. As the wind softly returned through the windows, Yesenia spoke, "You're such a disappointment. Esmeralda is a real woman. She's beautiful like me. She knows how to keep a man interested. You can only watch, wishing you were half the woman Esmeralda or I am."

Esperanza watched Yesenia's eyes search for submission, agreement with her delusion. After a moment, Esperanza smoothly responded, "You're right, Mama. Ezzy is like you. She's miserable. But unlike you, she knows it, and she has plans. I have a college degree and plans, too, and that means I'm not like you. You're right, I am better."

Yesenia's mouth dropped open, her eyes wide, shock waves washing through her, "You, … don't you, …." She searched, but had no answer for the truth. The mother drove home while the daughter stared out the passenger window, neither saying a word. Once in the carport, Yesenia pulled the door handle, declaring without looking at Esperanza, "I want you out of my house by next Sunday."

"Fine."

******

The hot day faded into a hot evening, warm winds still blowing up from the Gulf of California. Ezzy backed the Cadillac into a hospital parking space, "I'll wait here. Go up to the third floor, he's in room 338, Jaime knows you're coming."

"What about the nurses?" Espey cautiously asked.

"They're cool too. Don't take long. Get in, see him, say your prayers or whatever and get out. Okay?" Ezzy looked to Espey and reached out for her hand, "It's gonna be okay, but tonight's gotta be short, you understand?" Espey nodded as they held hands firmly, a moment of bonded understanding, knowing each heart's ache and wishing for something better.

The third-floor elevator doors swished open to subdued lighting, giving the lobby area a shadowy, dreamlike feel. Walking toward the nurse's station, Espey began looking for room numbers on the small plaques outside each door. Two nurses sat behind the counter working or writing, paying her no attention as she softly stepped by, looking first to them, then a room doorway, then back to them, then to another doorway. Finally, she saw a uniformed man sitting outside a room at the end of the hallway. As she approached, she watched him scrolling through his cell phone before he looked at her. Without making a sound, he watched her push the door open and slide by.

The room was dark, the reflective glare from parking lot lights drifted through the window to one wall. As Esperanza waited to let her eyes adjust, on the right side, the end of the bed became visible. The sounds of mechanical breathing hissed in rhythmic whispers, in

62

and out, in and out. She stepped past the room's private lavatory door and beheld Carl lying in the bed, his heavily bandaged head elevated, anesthetically unaware of beeps or lights or the tears sliding down Esperanza's cheeks.

Seeing him there, motionless, his life mechanically maintained, she remembered his smile, his profile in movie theater light, his eyes before he kissed her, faint images flowing across her mind of someone alive, someone she fell in love with. Remembering those moments, she steeled herself, forcing her steps, slowly, deliberately to the far side of the bed, away from the machines and wires, where ambient light would cover her like a shroud but show him fully. Standing there for a moment, she reached down and put her hand in his, lifting it gently.

"Carl, it's me. I'm here. I want you to hear me. I can only stay a few minutes, but I came to tell you, I love you. I'm going to be here when you wake up. I want you to wake up for me Carl, when you're ready." Now emotions started surging back and as she started quaking and feeling desperate. Her heart opened, "I need you to wake up baby, I want my life with you. I want us to have beautiful babies. I want you to take our babies to the movies. Please Carl, come back to me, okay?" Just then the door opened and Jaime stepped in. "Esperanza," he whispered, "It's time."

Looking to Jaime, she wiped the tears from her cheek and nodded. She looked back to Carl, "I'll be here when you wake up, I promise." Gently, she lowered his hand down to the bed and started towards the doorway, her eyes never leaving Carl's form until she was almost out of the room.

Returning to the car, Espey opened the door and sat down, her body convulsing with fear, her tears flowing. Ezzy reached across the center console and pulled her younger sister towards the middle, "Sh, sh, sh, it's gonna get better, you'll see."

"Oh, Ezzy I don't know! You should see him. He's got wires and tubes going in him. His head is wrapped like a giant ball. I'm scared, Ezzy." Espeys' shoulders quaked as her sobs grew louder, "Mama says I have to get out of the house by Sunday. What am I gonna do, Ezzy? What am I gonna do?"

Holding her sister, Esmeralda softly replied, "Sh, sh, I'll talk to Mama: you're not going anywhere."

******

Monday and Tuesday dragged for the women, even Marcos was bored. In order to manage the stresses and worries, Ezzy, Espey and Yesenia each took turns washing dishes, vacuuming, moping or sweeping, not just indoors but the patio, carport, front stoop and sidewalk. Ezzy sorted clothes in the boy's dressers and closets, filling two plastic garbage bags for donation. None of them could ever recall when they were all together for so long.

Wednesday morning, around nine o'clock while she was in the bathroom brushing her teeth, Ezzy's cellphone chimed. Rinsing her mouth, she picked up the phone and wiping her lips, asked, "Hello?"

"Ezzy, it's Maria."

"Hey, what's going on?"

"Tell your sister, her man's family is supposed to arrive today: they drove from Chicago. The doctors have been reducing his medication slowly, watching his brain. They think he might wake up today. Okay?"

"Yeah, thanks Maria." Esmeralda ended the call and went out to the hallway. Looking first at Yesenia's bedroom door, it was still closed. Ezzy then walked to the kitchen and saw Esperanza wiping the table while Abuela Carlotta rinsed dishes in the sink. Finishing their actions, Espey and Abuela Carlotta each poured a cup of coffee and sat down at the table.

Esmeralda followed them with her cup and sat last. A rare moment of comfort flowed to the girls as their grandmother smiled to each of them. In a soft tone Carlotta asked quietly, "So, what do you think you will do today?"

The sisters both looked out the sliding glass doors to the backyard and beyond, the morning's sunlight creeping over the trees and eastside chain-link fence. "I don't know what to clean next." Ezzy confessed, "I've done everything I can think of, if we had a dog, I might clean it too."

Carlotta and Esperanza each smiled, keeping their laughter under their chins. Watching her two granddaughters, the elder woman waited, sizing up their receptivity. After a moment, she started, "When did you stop dreaming?"

The question seemed to go unnoticed at first, each sister keeping her eyes fixed on the barren yard, the trees and sunlight. Ezzy then surprised the table, "When Arturo died, something in me died too."

Espey looked to Carlotta, "My dream got pulled back here and put somewhere." Then she asked, "Abuela, did you ever have any dreams?"

The small lady, her hair parted neatly down the middle of her crown, sipped her coffee. Holding her cup's rim with one hand, she brought the other to her chin. She now looked out to the daylight, her eyes peering through memories of long ago. Taking a deep breath, she held it briefly before remembering, "When I was about to graduate from high school, the first one in my family to do so, a man came to our town. He drove a truck, you know, like a bread delivery truck, only he took pictures in it." Now, she lifted her eyes to the ceiling, remembering the days.

"Did he take your picture, Abuela?" Ezzy asked softly.

"Yes, he took many pictures of me" she smiled, the memory still sweet decades later, "Mostly of my head, but, some of all of me."

"Abuela!" Espey gasped, "What did you do?"

The woman's eyes shone brightly, "I was attractive back then, I matured early like you," she nodded to Ezzy, "Many boys wanted me."

"I don't need to hear this," Ezzy objected.

"Sshh, I'm not ashamed, I did nothing wrong." Carlotta smiled, her eyes dropping down, her smile staying strong. "A week or so later, he came back and gave me an envelope. It had almost all the pictures he took, very big, some in color." She took another sip of coffee, now focusing on the memory hovering amidst the three women.

"And?" Ezzy asked, "What happened?"

Carlotta looked to the backyard, waiting briefly before continuing, "He said I should take them and go to Hollywood. He said girls like me, could work in movies. He gave me the phone numbers of agents to call." Her smile faded as her eyes held the memory in the air before her.

Esmeralda and Esperanza looked to each other, their minds reeling. Finally, Esperanza asked, "Abuela, did you go?"

Now the señora's noble chin quivered slightly, her eyes losing some of their gleam, "Yes, right after graduation. I snuck out my house one night and took a bus to Los Angeles."

"Oh my God," Esmeralda softly asked, "What happened?"

"After three weeks, I was homesick. I called some agents but nobody ever saw me. I felt foolish, so I took the last of my money and came back." The lady looked to her granddaughters, her eyes teary, "I let the world take my dream. I didn't try, I was too afraid."

"What happened when you came back home?" Esperanza asked respectfully.

"My father was very mad. He locked me in my room, letting me out only for breakfast and supper."

"He locked you in your room?" Esmeralda defiantly asked, "For what?"

"Salvador Mejia was a powerful man in our town. He was the supervisor of all the pickers. My father promised Salvador I would marry him right after high school." Now the elder woman's chin dropped down and her eyes no longer shone. The three women sat together in the resurrected humiliation. Taking one last sip, Carlotta quietly swallowed her coffee and memories, "I was afraid, I didn't try. I let those men decide my life." She exhaled, "But, I got your father, my beautiful Oscar, and now I have you two." She strained to smile, the effort's weight showing through.

"What happened to the pictures?" Esperanza asked.

Carlotta's smile faded away, "I burned them the day I got married."

The trio sat silently as the morning light grew across the yard. Carlotta rose first, putting her cup in the sink before she walked out to the carport to sit in her folding chair. Ezzy and Espey finished their coffee, not talking or thinking before Ezzy said, "Espey, come with me."

"What's up?"

Widening her eyes like a mother not to be challenged, she snapped her head toward the hallway, waving quickly. For a moment the two sisters stared at each other before Ezzy motioned again. Both walked quickly, silently down the hallway to their room where Ezzy entered and guarded the door as Espey passed through. Closing it quietly, Ezzy stepped within a foot of Espey and whispered, "They think he might wake up today."

"Really?" Esperanza's eyes now grew with excitement. "How do you know?"

"Maria called me, they been reducing the drugs to keep him asleep, watching his brain. She said they think he could wake up today."

As her smile emerged, Esperanza covered her mouth with one hand, slight tears forming. Her head shook up and down, understanding while her mind raced as she uttered, "I gotta get over there. I gotta be there when he wakes up."

"Whoa, whoa," Ezzy pushed her arms out to Espey's, clasping her forearms gently, "His family is coming from Chicago, they should be arriving today."

"So? Why does that matter?"

"Think." Ezzy looked directly to Espey, "They might not like you being there."

"Why not?" Espey suspiciously eyed her sister, not considering anything beyond seeing Carl awake.

"Well, he got shot in the restaurant you work in." Ezzy exhaled as she looked out the bedroom window. "People get weird when they don't know the whole story. They might think you're the reason he got shot."

"That's stupid!" Espey fired back, "I had nothing to do with Joaquin or those others." Espey now felt the heat building in her chest, "He was proposing to me," she started to whine, "why would I want him to get shot?"

"I know, I know, but these people, they've never seen you or anything. Who knows what they'll do when they see him lying there, you know?" Ezzy watched Espey closely, letting go of her arms and letting the moment breathe between them.

Wiping her cheeks, Espey sniffed as she looked out the window first, then back to her sister, "Ezzy, you're a great mom, but you're not my mom." Taking a deep breath, Espey turned to her dresser and pulled open a drawer to retrieve clean lingerie. Then she asserted, "I told him I would be there when he woke up. Now I'm going to take a shower, get dressed and go to the hospital." Briefs and bra in hand, she looked back to Ezzy, "Would you like to take me there so you can still have the car?" Swallowing deeply, Ezzy nodded and answered softly, "Sure."

At 10:15, Esperanza walked out from the elevator on the hospital's third floor. There were nurses and other people, some doctors, standing around or sitting behind the station counter. Remarkably, no one questioned her or asked who she wanted to see. Keeping her eyes forward, Espey walked while listening for someone's objection to her presence, it never came. She passed them all, her eyes focused down the hall where she noticed an empty chair, no one guarding room 338. The door to Carl's room was slightly ajar and she pushed it open further, slowly walking into a scene far different from what she remembered of Friday night's darkness.

Carl lay still on the bed, his head dressing much smaller. There was no tube down his throat. The intravenous line still connected him, but only to a single bag of clear fluid. The machine's beeps recorded his pulse, another line showing his blood pressure and a third told his oxygen level. But for the white gauze headband he appeared to be sleeping soundly.

A deep sense of gratitude filled Esperanza as she quietly sat down in the chair between the window and bed. He was breathing, he was still here, and he was still handsome, she would wait. Esperanza heard the multiple footsteps in the hallway but failed to perceive their distinction, they were getting closer and closer.

Suddenly, two lab-coated men halted at the doorway as a middle-aged woman and a tall, blond-haired man entered. The two men's coats identified them as "Dr." somebody, Espey didn't' see the last names. The woman stopped upon seeing Espey in the chair, her face solemn while her eyes searched Esperanza's. The blond-haired man stopped next to the woman, but he didn't look, focusing instead on Carl.

The woman was tall, with beautiful, shining, jet-black hair neatly brushed back and coming to her shoulders, showing an enviable widow's peak. Her skin had a luminous bronze-olive complexion, and her eyes were dark, piercing the light before them. She wore traditional white deck shoes and crisp, clean, tailored denim slacks, not blue jeans. An immaculately white golf-type short-sleeved shirt covered her torso, its collar snapped up under her hair with corners neatly pointing towards her shoulders. One hand, a gold watch on that wrist, held her purse. Her other wrist bore two thin gold bracelets, and her gold and diamond wedding ring sparkled like her eyes. That same hand clenched a white plastic bag. The woman's presence and beauty mesmerized Esperanza.

"Hello," one of the doctors started, "Who are you?"

Sitting fully erect, Esperanza replied, "I'm Esperanza Mejia. Carl is…"

"You're her." The woman stated, "Carl, this is her."

"Hmmn?" The tall blond man looked up from his son, "Who is this?"

"The girl he spoke about. Remember?" The woman's eyes stayed on Esperanza.

Feeling slightly dizzy at hearing this beautiful woman speak knowingly of her, Esperanza sat still as the blond-haired man turned to the doctors, "Listen, I parked in the entry circle, we rushed in to get up here." He looked to the beautiful woman, "I'm going to park our car, and then I'll be back, okay?"

The two doctors nodded, following the tall blond-haired man out of the room. As they left, the regal woman stepped forward to Esperanza, extending her hand to shake, "Hello Esperanza, I'm Caridad Cortez-Ralston, Carlos' mother."

Esperanza reflexively rose to the greeting, uncertain how to respond. Taking the manicured hand, she shook gently, respectfully, afraid of gripping to hard. "How do you do, I'm,"

"Esperanza, I know, you said that." The regal face softened to show warmth and confidence. "How long have you been here?"

"Uh, not long, I heard," she caught herself, "I mean, I just felt I should be here today." Espey looked to Carl, still sleeping, then back to Caridad, "Mrs. Ralston, I want you to know,"

"Call me Cari, please." Again, the smile beamed warmth and acceptance. Esperanza began to relax as the woman placed the plastic bag on the bed next to Carl's leg.

"I want you to know I'm very sorry this happened to Carl." Esperanza's stomach was flipping back and forth, her legs weakening, "I had nothing to do with the boy who did this." Esperanza started wringing her hands as she looked at Carl, her voice buckling slightly, "I'm sorry, I'm so sorry."

Cari watched the anguish in Esperanza. She waited a moment and then, taking a step closer, softly instructed, "Sit down dear, here," She backed Esperanza to the chair, "Sit down."

Esperanza sat down and held her forehead in one hand while Cari pulled the second chair closer to her. Once alongside, Cari sat down and leaned over, taking Esperanza's hand and holding it between Cari's soft and delicate hands. "I know all about you, my Carlos told me many times when he called. You're the girl of his dreams. You don't have to explain anything to me."

Cari's words fell ever so lightly into Esperanza's heart with the softness and beauty of floating cherry blossoms. She tried to imagine Carl describing her to this beautiful woman, but she suddenly felt embarrassed in her blouse, shorts, and sandals.

"He told you about me?" Esperanza's head spun again, a dizzying, swirling feeling making it hard to look at Cari's face. "What did he say?"

"Well, the last time we talked, he told me about this." She reached over and retrieved the white plastic bag. Inserting one hand, she shuffled around inside momentarily before withdrawing the navy blue box with gold trim. Setting the bag on the floor, Cari then turned the box once before opening its lid to reveal the gleaming white-gold engagement band and sparkling diamond. Turning it slowly left and right, she let the diamond's blues and whites and pinks flit about. Cari watched briefly before looking at Esperanza and sighing, "My son must love you very much."

Self-consciousness flowed over Esperanza. She bowed her head, hoping to hide her blush. The image of Carl extending the ring reappeared in her mind, his smiling eyes, the glow in his face. Happiness returned ever so lightly to her heart. Yes, she loved him too.

"So, Esperanza," Cari closed the box and sat back, "What is it about you that makes my son love you this much?"

"I wanted to be a teacher." Esperanza's slight joy waned when she realized her reality, "But after my father died, I had to come back and help my mother in the restaurant."

"Came back, from where?"

"College." Esperanza softly admitted.

"You have a degree?" Cari's tone was strong, more direct.

"Yes, Ma'am. Early education, K-through eight." Esperanza proudly replied.

Intrigued, Cari asked, "Where did you teach?"

"Oh, I didn't. I couldn't."

"Why not?" Cari's eyebrows knitted.

"I have my certificate, but I never got my license." Esperanza looked to the floor, feeling shame.

Cari listened intently. "Why didn't you get your license?"

Esperanza sighed heavily, now recalling the process. "In Colorado, you need two semesters of classroom teaching under a special new-teacher program. Once I completed that, I would get my license." She felt the weight of disappointment returning, "My mother insisted I come home right after graduation. Actually, she wanted me home before senior year." Esperanza looked to Cari, "But I stayed and got my degree." Esperanza waited for Cari's reaction, "She's resented me for that ever since."

A solemn pause filled the room as the two women looked to their love, sleeping peacefully, breathing easily, letting time move at a special pace. Watching Carl, Esperanza spoke softly, "Now, Colorado wants me to come to teach there. They say they'll give me ten thousand dollars for a house and a new teacher bonus and more for teaching in Spanish." She watched her love's chest move slowly up and down, the heart she coveted beating beneath. "They want an answer next week, and I don't know what to do."

Cari sat still, watching Esperanza struggle with an unfulfilled dream. Looking at Carl's form on the bed, Cari wandered back through her life, recalling the trail from her childhood to today, the faraway, remote differences that led her to herself.

"My father was a street vendor in Hermosillo. He walked miles every day selling Paletas. Do you know what those are?" Esperanza shook her head 'No'.

"They are the most wonderful fruit ice creams in the world." Cari's eyes brightened, and her face glowed as the joy from simpler times filled her heart. "He was happiest when he gave one to a *Niña pequeña*." She relaxed in the chair, "My mother died when I was ten, and my father struggled to care for me. He knew I loved to read and learn, but he couldn't provide all the things a young girl needs. So, he sent me to his cousins in Tucson."

Cari's tone became serious, the memories of harder times resurfacing, "I slept on a sofa on the back porch. They made me work in their restaurant, cleaning tables and washing pots and pans. They called me *'mula fea'* and laughed at me. Sometimes, on weekends, when I tried cleaning tables, some fat *'borochones'* would try grabbing my breasts or my butt. I hated it. They did nothing about it. My ancestors go back to the court of King Phillip II of Spain." She looked to Esperanza, rapt with attention, listening to every word. "I studied hard and got a scholarship to the University of Arizona. That's where I met Carl's father." Cari looked to the air before her, speaking to a vision only she held, "After I went to Tucson, I saw my father only once more, right before I went to college." Now her face took on a glow. "He told me how proud he was, how happy he was for me. He made me promise I would finish, be smart, be happy." Her voice softened, "He died in the street one day, selling Paletas, smiling at children."

The two women shared the silence, the machine beeps softly, comforting the room. After a moment, Carl Senior re-entered the room and walked to the end of the bed, his focus completely on his son. Cari inhaled deeply, "And then, after graduation, this marvelous man took me to Chicago and married me." She smiled broadly to her husband.

"And what do you do?" Esperanza asked softly.

"Me? Him?" Cari looked to Esperanza and then to Carl Sr., "I'm a high school principal, and he's a Superintendent." Her smile returned, beaming, her eyes sparkling. Sitting up fully in the chair, Cari clasped Esperanza's hand again, "So now, Esperanza Mejia, once my son wakes up, what are we to do?" Esperanza softly confessed, "He promised he'd take our babies to the movies."

Cari stiffened, "You're pregnant?"

"I don't know, maybe."

Carl Sr. looked to his wife, then Esperanza, his eyes working left to right and back. Taking a deep breath, Cari brought one index finger up, laying it over her upper lip. Silently, each person embraced the moment's providence right there in the room. Cari then proclaimed, "Well then, you'll have to come with us." The statement surprised Esperanza, "What do you mean?"

Looking to Carl Sr., Cari asked, "Do you know what Colorado is talking about?" Cari nodded toward Esperanza, "She has her teaching certificate but not her license. She says they're offering her a new teacher bonus and house money?"

He looked out the window, his mind searching, reviewing past conversations with state and federal authorities. Slowly, he started nodding, his lips pursed as he prepared his answer, "Yeah, I know about it. I'm sure we could do something like that." Carl Sr. asked Esperanza, "Can you teach in Spanish?"

Esperanza nodded, her eyes blinking as she shifted her body in the chair, "Yes, they said I could get thirty-five hundred a year more for that." Carl Sr. smiled knowingly, "I'm sure we offer more."

Now, the regal face of Caridad Cortez-Ralston returned as she calmly looked to Esperanza, "Good, then it's settled, you're coming with us. I won't have my grandson growing up here. The future's too uncertain." Esperanza's mind reeled as she could see her dream reforming before her. Cautiously, she asked, "What if it's a girl?"

Carl Jr's leg suddenly twitched, sliding out to the edge of the bed and back into the center. He exhaled as he tried lifting one arm off the bed. Turning his head away from the bright window light, he opened his eyes. His throat dry, voice scratchy, he whispered, "Mom, hey."

The other three stood transfixed, seeing their prayers answered before them. Stunned and curious, they waited, hoping to see Carl Jr.'s complete return. Esperanza repeated Cari's words in her head while focusing her attention on Carl Jr. Cari stood up and leaned over, touching Carl Jr.'s leg, "I'm right here, baby. How're you feeling?"

Cari waited for Carl Jr.'s response, and after hearing nothing, she looked to Esperanza, "Do you want your daughter growing up here?"

Carl Jr.'s eyes opened slightly. Looking at Esperanza, he whispered, "I knew you'd be here." He smiled, closing his eyes again. Esperanza stepped to Carl Jr.'s side, and as she took his hand, she looked to Cari, "Can my sister and nephews come too?"

Both Carl's replied, "Of course."

Esperanza smiled to Cari, "When do we leave?"

Adam & Eve

G. E. Russell

The jeep caromed down the roadway, dust streams spiraling from its rear, rising up, floating into the air, disappearing in seconds. Two passengers lifted and sat in response to the dips and swerves, each holding something tightly to keep them close to their seats, his hands on the steering wheel, hers on the canopy frame and seat.

"How much further?" she called.

"Not much, just a bit more." He replied.

The sun beamed high overhead, desert heat now flushing away the last moments of morning cool. Dry, and isolated, the remote path wound onward, to their left, eternal mountains watching. Scrub, and cacti, many of them in various sizes, shapes and faded greens, dotted the eastward landscape. Distant clouds, and occasional blotches of refreshing whiteness hovered here and there, somewhere far away from wherever.

"Here we go!" He proclaimed, slowing down slightly to turn right, off the roadway onto the sand, rolling down toward the greenery, away from the last evidence of order, into the pristine, sacrosanct geography of endless openness. Downshifting the transmission, he let the clutch out to feel the lower gear's pull as he guided the wheels between prickly pear and barrel cacti.

She was surprised at the sand's firmness, no sinking or sliding, instead rolling smoothly like on a billiard table. She relaxed her grip on the seat's left edge, her right hand still clinging firmly to the canopy frame above her. She exhaled, long and smooth, the slower pace reassuring her. She looked at the panorama to her right, something akin to a calendar photograph, erratic edges and shapes, sporadic gaps between sage, green, or brown areas, blond sand beneath, and a distant horizon under a brilliant blue sky. Nothing more in any direction, nothing unseemly, nothing unnatural. Nothing.

"Where are we?" she asked, scanning the front, then back, then all around.

"Nowhere"

"And where are we going?"

"Nowhere"

She balked, this made no sense, "Why are we going nowhere if we're already there?"

"To get there, we have to get away from here, from everything."

"Have you been here before?" Her eyes searched his face.

He grinned, "Nope. I've been nowhere before, found nothing, but not the nothing here, not this nowhere." Sifting his coded response back and forth, she watched his fervor, driving hell-bent to somewhere neither one of them had ever been to. He steered smoothly, weaving the tires over the sand, a humming coming up through the chassis. "You'll see, you'll see when you quit looking for what you think you need."

"Like what?"

"Like why? Or when or how? This will be different. You'll see if you let yourself."

"What will be different? Me? You?" She waited, holding her breath.

He let the moment float, his grin softening, a resignation to organized thinking before responding, "We get trained to rely on things that restrict us, hold us in some place, keep us focused on the next ten or twenty minutes ahead, ignoring everything else, shapes, colors, sounds, life itself." He looked to his left, off to the mountains, "I can't stand it. It's like being eaten alive."

She wondered how shapes and colors could be missed, how life could be overlooked? Watching him return his focus ahead, she cautiously asked, "When did you first think this?"

"Fifty years ago, I rode my motorcycle out into the desert." He let a faint memory of long ago come to the front of his mind, "I parked it, got off and walked, walked until I had to stop. I stopped, took off all my clothes, piled them on my boots and started walking again. I went until I wanted to sit down, and I did."

"Then what?"

"That was the start." He swerved the jeep left, avoiding a large flat rock cooking a diamondback rattlesnake. It leaped at the front tire, missing the vehicle completely before slithering quickly into the sand and foliage. She watched, fascinated by its speed, fluidity, and ever-shifting shape. Her mind returned to the image of him sitting alone in the desert, naked, "Then what happened?"

"A realization came to me, like rising slowly to a height where you could see everything laid out before you, smoothly, requiring no energy or effort."

She listened intently, "And what did you see?"

His smile returned, his teeth uniform, shining, "Nothing. Everything."

Ten minutes of silence swirled around them as the jeep wove left and right, straight before veering one way, then back. Lifting his foot off the accelerator, he let the vehicle roll to a stop.

"We're far enough." He looked around three-hundred sixty degrees, the white broad-brimmed hat covering his head, Ray-Ban aviator sunglasses reflecting the open range, his hand rubbing his chin.

He reached for the top button on his linen shirt, plucking it open and proclaiming, "Come on, this is it."

She gasped, "You sure?"

"Yep, this is where you want to be, trust me."

She looked behind, first over her left shoulder, then her right. Looking back at him she saw his chest, the silver-white hairs, bristling, covering both his nipples, his broad belly, freckles across his upper arms flowing down to his wrists. His shirt landed on the driver's seat and after he unbuckled his belt, he bent over, sliding his shorts and underwear down to his feet. Holding on to the steering wheel, he stepped back, away from the clothing. The shorts and underwear came to the seat and he stood in sandals, a hat and sunglasses, his head tilted back, facing up to the sun, his smile broad under his mustache.

She watched in silent amazement, he was so brazen, so certain despite the surroundings. He turned and walked out in front of the jeep grill where he stopped and faced the open terrain before him, widened his stance, and extended both arms upward, fists clenched, a human "X" commanding attention as a roar came up through his loins and belly and heart into a voice of exuberance and elation, "YYEEAAAHH, God I've needed this!"

Holding his stance, he let the sun slather every pore, a subtle wisp of air casually flowed over them, holding the moment. She listened to the soft rustle of sage and juniper leaves whispering refreshing calm.

Letting his arms down slowly, he turned to her, "Well, what are you waiting for?"

"Oh, I don't know, I, …"

"Come on, you said you'd do it, believe me, you'll love it."

"I know what I said, but this is rather sudden."

"It is not!" he objected, "I've been waiting years for this."

"I know you've talked about it, but why must it be like this?"

He stood there in full view, his body gallantly displaying seventy-two years of wear, proud shoulders and biceps now smaller, a rotund midsection, thighs once powerful, now deflated, hovered above knobby knees, his smile advancing from the softened jawline. He stepped to her side, extending one hand, "Come on,"

"Is this really necessary?" she whined.

"Yes, for us to be us, it's necessary."

She looked about wondering as she stepped down to the hard sand. A slight edge of shade hung to her side and she looked to him, his smile reassuring her, "There's no one out here, just us."

Slowly, she unbuttoned the floral print blouse, a soft weave fabric, airy, light. It went to her seat, and she reached behind to unclip her bra. He marveled at her full breasts, still exciting him, neither age nor life diminishing their promise of comfort. The bra landed on the blouse and she looked around again. Now her fingers went to the waistband of her shorts, where a large white button stood out against the light blue denim. Slipping it through the opening, she unzipped the shorts, letting them fall to her ankles. Again, she looked to him, twisting her face, "Can't I leave my underwear on?"

"No, no," he shook his head, "you need to be completely free, away from everything we've been taught was normal. We don't have to be afraid, what you're about to feel is beyond understanding or explaining."

She listened, he smiled and stood still. They waited momentarily before she relented, "Oh, alright."

She pulled the light panties down and grasped them and her shorts together, stepping out and putting them on the seat. Standing upright, she became the female bookend in sandals, wide-brimmed hat and sunglasses. She looked at him, his smile even broader, his face radiant.

"Take it in for a minute," he said. Placing his hands on his hips, he eyed her, her ample bosom, a white, soft belly, slightly pouched by time and motherhood, her hips and buttocks newly introduced to burning light, her tan showing just above her knees, washing down to her toes. "Don't look at me," he said, "look out there, everywhere, wherever you like."

She turned her head slowly, sweeping in the vista before her. It was beautiful in its own strange and unique way. Another whisper of dry air crossed her torso, relaxing her. Her breathing slowed as her hands came to her hips and she noticed different shapes and nuanced colors, colors she didn't think possible in the desert. He let her absorb it all, keeping quiet, watching her, waiting. The breeze returned while a stronger wind, out in front by one hundred yards, sent a dried tumbleweed bounding across the open space.

"It's awfully hot out here."

"It won't matter, you'll see when we get there."

"You mean we're not there now? How much further do we have to go? The sun's burning everything."

"Don't worry." And he opened the glove box in the jeep. Fishing about with his hand a moment, he smiled again when pulling out the colored plastic tube of sunscreen, "Here we go."

She cupped her hands as he squeezed a small white puddle into them. As she spread the lotion across her arms, then forehead and cheeks, he stepped behind her and began wiping her shoulders and down her back. Slight folds of flesh, unprotected for some time, absorbed the emollient swiftly, disappearing after one or two swipes. His large hands ran down the small of her back and across each buttock, to the fold just above each thigh. He covered each side under her ribs, again, the calloused hands covered soft skin around her hips and down, her belly soothed by the cooling lotion. She thought of moments long ago, when his caress inflamed her senses, pulling her, delivering soft ecstasy that suspended time, a sensation of lightness.

Taking another handful of balm, lost in the faraway moment, she began covering his shoulders as he leaned toward her abdomen, his hands wiping her flesh, her breasts, down to her upper thighs, and back up to her clavicles. Closing her eyes, she let her arms extend to his lower back, softly weaving back and forth between a memory of his virile youth and the welcome comfort of his mature frame.

Standing to wipe his chest, he bathed in light and gel, hairs front and back glistening. As he wiped the back of his neck, she returned the favor of protecting his buttocks. Bending down, she covered his hips, upper thighs and loins, slowing her pace, letting her hands simply touch the softer areas. In silence, they indulged themselves beyond a simple physical interaction. Instead, they savored the pure eroticism of merely touching one another softly, lovingly. "We could let ourselves finish this moment right here. It would be enough for me."

He smiled patiently, "We could miss everything too."

As the last precautions were applied to feet and toes, the cap was snapped on the tube and it returned to the glove box. He stood up and looked to her, his smile again radiant, "Ready?"

She nodded and he extended his right hand to her. Clasping it, they walked forward into the open arena, only the sound of their sandals twisting against the sand beneath them.

"How far will we go?" she asked.

"As far as we feel, then we'll come back."

"How will we know our way back?"

He smiled broadly, "We'll stop when we want, take a deep breath, then turn about and follow our tracks."

Now her smile flowed forth, "Of course."

In the beginning, their pace was moderate, relaxed, they strode side by side, holding hands for about three hundred yards.

"Are you trying to teach me something?" She coyly asked.

"Maybe you already know, but forget." He smiled.

"I don't like the sound of that." She looked out to the mountains.

After a quarter-mile, his determination pulled him ahead of her, leading a charge to something neither could see and only he felt. Breathing became harder, each step pushing tendons and muscles, heat rising through sandals, igniting toes and heels. The heat and exertion brought perspiration to armpits, necks, inner thighs and elsewhere, causing occasional beads of sweat to roll down one's back or temple. As the daylight broiled their surroundings, they stopped, and panting heavily, she admitted, "Whew, this is something."

"You okay?"

"We should've brought some water." Her panting started to slow.

"It won't be long. Look, there's a path," he pointed over her shoulder to a small hill. She turned and looked, "Where?"

"To the left, over there. See it?"

She looked again and shook her head, "No." She waited a moment, but he didn't. Another ten minutes of marching through sage, Pricklypear and Saguaro cactus, the random gecko suddenly darted off a rock, away down the trail or between them, left or right. She looked to the sky, burnished a bright blue by the relentless sun.

"Are we close?" She called, stopping and waiting for his response. He walked onward three more steps before looking back to her. He stopped, panting, his rib cage expanding and contracting, shoulders rising and sagging, "What?"

She bent forward, putting her hands on one knee, "How much further?"

He walked back to her, stopping three feet away, watching her breathing hard, his exhalations almost perfectly timed to hers, "You want to quit?"

"This is about the party, isn't it." She challenged.

"No, that's long over." He looked to the mountains.

"I said I was sorry, many times."

"I know. This isn't about anything like that. I've moved on."

"To what?" She bit her lip, anxiously waiting, breathing hard.

"I've realized women, some, want to manage their pains and their passions."

"And men?"

He faced her directly, "Men don't care to manage anything. They'd rather control everything." He returned his gaze to the horizon, "I've realized I can't do either. But I've got a chance to be happy."

"Doing whatever this is we're doing?"

Nodding in the open air, "Uh-huh, this is where I can find it." He looked to her again, "You can too, if you let yourself."

"You're retaliating." She charged.

"Nope, I'm getting my soul back."

Gulping twice, she shook her head, "No, no, I just, …. What are you looking for?"

He looked around behind her to the mountains in the distance, the haze softening their edges in layers of blue or purple. Stepping to her right, he walked around her, looking to the horizons, west, north and back east, the sun's glare washing every solid object into soft form. He paced evenly until back at her left side, looking south. Watching her shadow move slightly upward, she asked, "Is this nowhere enough?"

"C'mon," He started again, walking away from her, down a shallow and back on the path. Doggedly, he marched on, almost invisible from ten feet away. The path wound and wandered up gradually between low shrubs, small cacti and rocks, some as large as garbage cans, strewn a respectful distance from the Saguaros. She followed, looking to his backside every fourth or fifth step.

"Do you feel it?" he called over his shoulder.

"Feel what?"

"The freedom."

"From what?"

"Everything, clothing, mankind, convention, life as we're told it should be."

Pacing her steps, shorter, more directly aligning ankle, knee, and hip joints, she watched the trail and confessed, "I'm not sure what my butt's feeling right now."

He laughed back, "No? Just let go! Let go of all you think!" Moving forward, he was panting, his arms swinging with his steps, his back glistening with moist, silver hairs, shining in the sunlight. She followed his footprints, not looking to the hilltop, not stopping to see the far horizon, working to keep his pace, his steps sounding softer and softer until she couldn't hear them.

Looking up from the ground before her, she saw him, eighty feet or so ahead at the hilltop, hands on hips, looking to the far mountains, his smile again broad.

"Tell me again why we live in a city?" He questioned.

She arrived at the hilltop to his left, panting, bending over, placing her hands above her knees, thinking about the question, breathing deeply, the warm air drying her nostrils and throat. After a moment, she stood up, "We wanted to enjoy life?"

"And what does that mean?"

 "Home, our kids, friends, things we like." She offered.

"We could've had those anywhere. What did we need with civilization?"

She wrinkled her face, her nose twisting as if confronted by a foul odor, "Should we live in the wilderness?"

"Look at this, right here, right now," He commanded, twisting slightly at the waist, sweeping his eyes from left to right, "this is life, right here."

"Whatever do you mean?" She asked.

He stepped forward a little further and as he sat down, cross-legged, he extended his hand, "Come here, sit with me."

She walked to his side then stopped, "I'm all sweaty," she whined, "it's sand and rocks."

"Sit, sit and calm your mind, any sand will dry and fall off during our walk back."

Obediently, she took his hand and gently let herself down to the ground, again surprised by its firmness, not as gritty or invasive as she feared.

Exhaling fully, she asked, "Now what?"

His hands on his knees, he stared out to the mountains possibly twenty miles away, shaded by the light blue haze of atmosphere. The wind again touched them both, lightly, silently cooling them. She listened to the wind's whisper under the brim of her hat, felt grains of sand cross her forearms and knees. She watched the clouds peacefully float miles above. It was ethereal, a transition from all things that daily retard the spirit, corrode the soul.

"We put ourselves in a trap," He announced. "A wheel we keep running in and never getting anywhere. We get up, go to work, a job, a church on Sunday and never know how we fit in the universe. We never stop to align with the rest of existence, knowing so little about ourselves. We think we're in control, but we're not."

Her gaze drifted out to the horizon, she thought about how she'd gone through life thinking of herself separate from the universe. Being a mother, a wife, a person with needs and fears, *that*, she believed, was the universe. She never considered invisible forces or relations to aspects of life and whether or not they made her happy.

He continued, "We're part of something so much larger than ourselves and we rarely understand that. Instead, we get caught up in living to avoid thinking about death." With a lower, solemn voice he asked, "Do you feel it?"

She listened further, a slight touch of breeze, the air moving but not forcing, "Feel it?"

"Here, in the center, right here, right now."

"Center? Here?"

"We're at the center of our universe darling. Right here, right now, you and me and the entire universe accepts us." His gaze, posture, his entire being relaxed, serene, accepting the light, the heat, the wind. He smiled again, "It's all here for us, holding us and we're free, nothing stopping us, blocking us."

She looked to the horizon again, her eyes examining the distance, the shapes, the colors. She stopped thinking of her joints, her skin or any perils, instead feeling herself lighter, her mind accepting the surrounding light. She professed, "You're really happy right now, aren't you?"

She marveled at the bond she now felt, a much deeper confidence, "I don't think I've ever seen you like this."

He smiled, nodding while staring ahead, calmly breathing, at peace. He looked different, not just a handsome man, not a spouse, he was somehow transformed, her partner by extension, from him, of him, with him. She thought to herself, *'Remember this feeling, this lightness, nothing to worry about, just him and me. The sun, the stars and the moon, they're all with us, him and me and we belong here.'*

Her breathing slowed, her heart liberated, beating confidently. Closing her eyes, she welcomed this new calm, a feeling she'd never experienced before. She was curious but didn't want to disturb the peace swirling about her and coming out from deep within. She felt the airflow, not caring for more than this moment. She quickly glanced to him, motionless, palms open to the sky, deep slow breaths barely visible. Her wonder overtook her, "Is it always like this? I mean, when did you figure this out?"

His head bobbed slightly, "Every time." His eyes remained closed, "Fifty years ago, the first time. I felt this and foolishly went on, thinking I'd find similar happiness elsewhere. I've searched for it ever since." He looked to the clouds, the light and beyond, "I've never felt more alive than right now."

She basked in the sunlight covering her, the heat now comforting her, her mind drifting in the delicate wind holding her soul aloft. Seeing a bird far away, effortlessly gliding in the wind, she said aloud, "We're free, just being here, everything with us, moving around us, through us."

He turned to her for a moment, then stood up. Reaching for her hand, he lifted her to him, wrapping his arms around her completely, pressing her into his chest. Their lips met in full closure, passion powering their kiss, a passion seasoned by years of loyalty, friendship, shared joys and heartaches. Now, under the glaring sun that passion returned pure.

He held her close, their sweat smoothed surfaces moving evenly, effortlessly, as their embrace twisted them closer and closer. Her passion surging, she extended her arms to the small of his back, then upward over the once broad muscles, coming to his shoulders as her hips lifted slightly to his. Ending their kiss, he exclaimed, "God, I love you."

She smiled back, "I never thought I could love you more, but here, now, I love you more than ever." Like a small child craving approval, he asked, "This is how we're meant to be. Don't you think?"

"I do, I do, we should've done this long ago."

"Well, we've done it now. There's no going back."

"No. And we shouldn't." She asserted.

"Never again. We know better."

"Yes, yes we do."

Encore Collision

G. E. Russell

"Let's get this over with," I muttered to the air.

The other three looked to me as they started walking toward a sleek black extended Lincoln limousine, the standard vehicle for these times. I took the back seat, right side, to look out the opera window while we traveled. Conceding my spot, the others entered and sat quietly.

"How long's this gonna take?" Joey asked.

"Why?" Tommy, my best friend replied, "You got somewhere else to go?"

"No."

"Not that long, who cares, it's the last one."

Shaking his head as he reached for a glass on the bar, Randy's bent torso blocked my forward view. Pulling tongs from the ice bucket, he placed cubes in the glass. Stopping after three, he looked around, "Am I the only one drinking?"

Tommy Richards, our lead guitarist, looked at me while Joey the keyboardist, yawned, "Nah, not me man."

I watched Tommy and Randy before deciding to be the adult, "Randy, it's not even one o'clock."

Like a high schooler repeating an inside joke, he smirked, "That makes a difference?"

The driver slid into the front seat and pulled on his seat belt. He looked into the rear-view mirror and called out, "Everybody ready?"

A trio of tired and indifferent, "Yeahs" came back and he pulled the gearshift lever down. The vehicle's lurch helped Randy flop back into the side bench as wheels turned, moving the black behemoth forward. Pulling out of the parking lot, the driver slowed, looked right, then left and accelerated. The surge into traffic pushed my mind back through decades to the day this madness started. As we rolled forward, faint images of long ago flashed.

******

I was fifteen years old, scrawny, tormented by acne and anonymity. Tommy called me over to his house one Saturday, saying he was forming a band and needed a drummer. This was answered prayer for two reasons. First, I needed to get out of my house before my father found work for me. Second, rock and roll bands were the hottest thing in high school, surpassing football and basketball, two cultures completely foreign to me. Girls came to any event offering live music, good or bad. I manically practiced my drums for hours without prodding or limit. Sitting next to our Zenith stereo, my lust to perform with every rock band went beyond a simple fascination. I poured over album covers and credits the way other teenage boys ogled Playboy playmates.

Once at Tommy's, we went out to his garage where, Lance DeMars sat on a bar stool strumming a sunburst guitar. He stopped when we walked through the side door. Ambient daylight from three small windows and a fluorescent light hanging over the work bench were our only illumination. Silently, I waited for my eyes to adjust as the odor of gasoline, oil and grass clippings entered my nostrils.

"This is Tim Walsh, the drummer I told you about" Tommy announced. Lance sat slowly strumming before shifting his attention away from the fretboard. I watched Lance sit mute, unresponsive. I remember feeling confused when Tommy asked, "Did you bring your drums?"

"No."

92

"Man, how we gonna practice without your drums?"

"Tommy, you said come over, you didn't say we're going to practice."

"What kind of a drummer travels without his drums?" Lance looked at me like I was the dumbest person on earth. Before I could answer he followed, "You *are* a drummer, right?"

"Yeah,"

"You any good?" Lance's trademark sneer crept up one corner of his mouth.

"You a drummer?" I replied. The smirk dropped as his strumming slowed, his eyes fiery before his lips bounced. "No."

"Then you wouldn't know a good drummer from a bad one, would you?" I looked to Tommy, his hands stuffed into his back pockets.

"Look, guys," Tommy started, "let's figure out what we want to do. We'll practice during the week."

"Can't do it man. My old man won't let me out on a weeknight." Lance shook his head as he tried tuning the fifth string. It whined flat to sharp and back as he searched for the correct note. Twisting the peg back and forth for fifteen seconds, he landed back on the original tone. "Besides, *I* got this gig for Friday night. I need a band, not just some guys."

It was right there I first experienced Lance's arrogance. His dismissive tone, never looking at us while talking, focusing instead on his guitar. I remembered thinking, '*This guy's an asshole.*'

******

Our limo merged into the center lane under sizzling southern California daylight. Another Los Angeles day, omnipotent sunlight and endless traffic. We're all comfortable in our detached and cocooned reality, growing up viewing life through limousine or tour bus windows. Looking to the sidewalks, I saw people stepping between shade and sunlight, walking through their lives, unaware of our fame, fatigue or whatever holds us.

"How long's it going to take to get there?" Joey asks the driver.

"With this traffic, forty-five minutes at least."

"Sheesus,"

I call to Randy, "Any bottled water in that bar?"

He nods, pulls one out and tosses it to me. Cracking the plastic cap, I swig a mouthful and recall a six-ounce Coke bottle at that first gig. As I swallow, I see the sign, 'Bill's Diamond Tap' hanging outside, baking in the sunlight and my early memories continue. Lance demanded we show up at seven o'clock, swearing we'd be done by ten. For our first set we played eight songs, badly, three we'd actually rehearsed Wednesday night. It was my high school sophomore spring and the Friday night birthday party was on the second floor of the Times Lounge.

We'd practiced less than an hour because Lance lied, telling his dad he was going to the library. Lance's father, Henry, was an ex-Marine who thought rock and roll stupid and the Beatles communist deviants. Once Henry went ballistic over Lance's playing *She Loves You* on his acoustic at home. After that, Lance kept his electric guitar a secret at Tommy's house.

Me on the other hand, I was lucky. My father, also a veteran of the big one, was also a drummer, working part-time playing with different groups around town. He didn't care for the Beatles either, but limited his disapproval to keeping my hair short. We fought over other issues, frequently avoiding one another for days, but music was our invisible coupling.

******

While waiting for the light to change, Joey asks, "What's going on later?" We all shrug before I reply, "Some people are getting together at the studio."

Randy swallowed another gulp of scotch, then asked, "Suits gonna be there?"

"Yep," Tommy nods. We all look away as if hearing our least favorite relative was on the phone. The limo slows to a stop and I look ahead as people cover the crosswalk en masse and I remember the Times bar manager. As we ended the first set, he came upstairs, "People are watching the ball game. They can't hear the TV. Turn it down." He turned away and rumbled down the stairway. Lance's jaw set and he purposely turned up the volume on his guitar. He started the second set blasting away. I watched, waiting for someone to tell Lance to ease up. By the song's end the manager was back, telling us to pack up and get out.

The birthday girl's parents negotiated a second chance. I suspected once Lance got another bite of the manager's apple, he'd spit it out. After the parents said, "Keep it down." Lance sat on a chair and refused to play. When the parents turned their backs, he flipped them off. My very first gig included a textbook, narcissistic temper tantrum.

******

I take another swig of water as Tommy slides over to me, "What'ya thinkin' man?"

"Nothin', just want to get this over and go home."

"Well, after this, we'll have time. Wanna go somewhere?"

I look back out the window, shaking my head, "We just came off a six-month tour and you wanna travel?"

"Man, it's not like we're playing or anything."

"I'll need some space man, some quiet."

Rolling steadily, we passed a dry-cleaner, and I watched a woman walking out, one arm extended up, holding up three or four items on hangars. The plastic sheath fluttered in the breeze as she brought the lower edges up in a fold. Pastel colors under the polyethylene reminded me of the night we played a country club poolside. I look to Tommy, "Remember that night we played at Bel-Mar, the wedding reception by the pool?"

Tommy searched his memories, then shook his head 'no.'

"Remember, a thunderstorm started, we all thought we'd be electrocuted?"

Tommy searched again, his eyes sliding left to right, "You mean when Lance nailed the bride?"

"Wasn't that Bel-Mar?"

Tommy's face softened and his smile formed as he pushed his hair back, his hand stopping at his hairline. "Yeah, we looked for tablecloths or tarps to cover the amps and he disappeared. Remember?"

I recalled the night clearly, "Then he came back in that clear plastic raincoat?"

"Yeah! He came out wearing just his pants and that raincoat." Tommy started laughing, then coughing, his deep, wet cough releasing, "The groom and the bride's old man wanted to kill him."

"I did too, they said they weren't going to pay us and my drums were soaked."

We paused in the memory. Decades of travel, music and memories held us in stages. Lance fired a bunch of musicians but kept Tommy and I with him, repeatedly telling us we'd thank him someday. Now, he's got us doing one last show, finishing a grinding six-month tour. One hundred and fifteen shows in one hundred and eighty-six days.

Lance kept repeating, "Everything will be first-class man, it'll be freakin' great!"

I had doubts. Over forty years I'd seen enough, I'd lost interest long ago in watching Lance's act night after night. Make no mistake, when inspired, Lance put on a killer show. From that first gig in the Times Lounge, when girls stood staring at him, mesmerized as he sang. We were invisible, immaterial to Lance, we just didn't know it.

******

The light changed to green and we started rolling again. Another six blocks, an angular turn and we merged onto the highway. Once again, we're rolling to our next show. Time has always been measured by our arrival, performance and departure to the next venue. Feeling the limo moving faster, conversation volumes increased.

"Hey Tom," Randy asks, "was Lance's second wife Darlene or Linda? I could never keep em' straight." He looks to Tommy and Joey for an answer.

"Linda," says Joey.

"No," Tommy sparks, "He just dated Linda. She won't be there." Tommy looked to me, "Right?"

"What? He and Linda weren't married?" Joey scratched his head, turning to Randy, "I thought they got married."

Tommy cleared his throat loudly and looked at them both over his sunglasses.

Linda was my wife. She and Lance had an affair for about two years. We'd cut our third album and were touring when she overdosed. I hadn't paid attention to her drug use or the times she and Lance were out of my sight. I never confronted Lance. I liked the life I had, the life he took me to. But after the affair, I never got past hating him. I thought back to the night she overdosed and how we all slept in the hospital waiting room. Leaning toward Tommy, I asked his left ear,

97

"Where were we when she OD'd? St. Louis? Kansas City? Somewhere in the Midwest, right?"

Cruising now, the limo is doing at least eighty-five. Joey announced he needed a scotch, so Randy prepared another glass. After giving Tommy a can of ginger ale, he hands him a glass with ice. Tommy pops the tab and pours the golden liquid. The frothing hiss subsided as Tommy put the can between his legs.

"You heard from her? How's she doing?" Tommy asks me, turning more to his right to face me. I also shift to talk with him quietly.

"I talked to her the other night. She's doing good. Lives near Chicago now." He nodded while taking another sip, and after swallowing, said, "Good for her."

We sat together silently watching the world beyond the pavement streak by, a fluid blur of faded colors under bleaching sunlight. Tommy turned back, "How about you? How you doing?"

I lifted my water bottle, "Fifteen years, one day at a time."

Tommy nodded, lifting his ginger ale, "My man."

After my divorce, I spent six months drinking, touring and taking out my anger on everybody, everywhere, every way. Tommy got fed up and dragged me to an AA meeting. Later I learned he did that to pacify Lance, who wanted me out of the band. Some balls, huh? He destroyed my marriage and wanted me fired for being mad.

Tommy's smile broadened, his head nodding, the limo moving us forward. I pondered my life of traveling, performing, and struggling with things I'd never encountered before. When seen night after night from an arena stage or day after day through tinted tour bus windows, the world is surreal. Now, my career filters every day, a vocation that demands I retain my youth. Exhausted, we've all become jaded by the economic realities of aging while carrying the weight of success. We've grown beyond frustrated trying to sound fresh, exuberant, innocent. Once I tried thinking of me doing some other job, but couldn't see any path. Besides, the money's just too damn good.

******

Passing a pro sports arena, I recalled the performance that made us known. Randy turned to Tommy and me, "Isn't that where we opened for Springsteen?" I lean forward to look out the door window. Tommy leaned forward too and we looked at each other. Tommy looked to the arena, "I dunno, maybe." He turned to me, "Whad'ya think?"

I smile, "No, but it looks like it, doesn't it? We opened for Springsteen in Orange County." I looked to the light coming through my small opera window and remembered Lance taking us there three hours before the show. Walking out on stage, I couldn't see the back of the arena. I wondered if the other guys would hear me while playing. The platform was much larger than the entire Times Lounge. Randy and I looked at each other, our mouths gaping in awe. Tommy walked to the stage's edge, put one hand over his eyebrows and peered into the darkness, an endless nothing. Echoes, solitary lights beyond the stage, an empty canyon waiting for Bruce, the E Street Band and maybe us. I remembered Lance proclaiming "I'm gonna tell the world Stonecraft is here to kick your ass!"

We warmed up that crowd, way up, and maybe they warmed us up too. After all, Springsteen and E Street were following. Maybe they cheered just to get us off the stage. I didn't know and didn't care. I remembered feeling simultaneously on fire and ice cold. Nothing could touch us, we were on our way. I remembered Lance, his face glowing, eyes wide. I remembered thinking, *I wonder if Henry knows about this?'* I knew the answer instantly.

Later that night, I was dumbfounded when I opened our hotel room door and there stood Steve Van Zandt and Clarence Clemons. Lance invited them in, and Tommy offered his chair to Clarence. We guffed and stammered like school kids for about fifteen minutes while they drank their beers before saying, "Thanks, we gotta go."

Lance left with them as we sat amazed, blinking at one another. Rock and roll royalty just left our room. For the first time I began to see how Lance's fixation on fame and success touched me. But nothing was assured, twenty minutes later, Lance returned with three high school-aged girls. A minute later, he lit a joint and offered it to them. I pulled him in the bathroom, "Lance, are you nuts? How old are those girls?"

He looked at himself in the mirror, "Who cares?"

"Tell me one of ems' *at least* eighteen."

Watching the mirror, his expression never changed, focusing completely on himself. His eyes glowed red around the edges. His smile morphed into a snarl as he slowly nodded his head. I realized the pot was a cover, but I wasn't sure for what. Exhaling a jetliner-like vapor trail he told his reflection, "Okay, no pussy for Tim."

After rinsing his hands, he wiped them on a towel and walked out to the room. I told my reflection, "Don't touch any of them."

******

We've spent forty years together, cocooned in vehicles like this one, believing we were entitled to our efforts, our creativity, and our abilities to entertain. But it's none of that today. It's a rolling sarcophagus in which we escape from real life. The limo slithered through traffic quietly, carrying us outside society, outside life. I look ahead and watch Joey and Randy talking to one another, then to Tommy whose head was back against the top of the seat. I nudged him and he turned to me, "What?"

"When do you think Lance first started using heavy?"

"What'ya mean?"

"More than pot and booze." I continued.

"Shit, he was hardcore in high school."

"What?"

Pushing his sunglasses back up the bridge of his nose. Tommy nodded and sighed, "Yeah, he was doin' mescaline, acid, junior year, I think. Definitely senior year."

I thought I knew our collective histories, but couldn't recall one instance in high school when I suspected Lance, "No way."

"For real man," Tommy leaned forward, motioning for Randy to put more ice in his glass. "His old man would ground him for, god, anything. Lance had connections who'd stop by and toss shit up to his bedroom window. Remember that little bedroom window?"

I thought back to the house Lance grew up in, a small one-and-a-half-story bungalow featuring two main floor bedrooms, one for his parents and one for sister Beth. The upstairs had two dormer rooms made from the converted attic. Each room had two windows, one facing south toward the street and one to either the east or west side. The side window was only eighteen inches or so- wide, too small for an air conditioner and barely big enough for Lance to slip through when I placed the extension ladder up to it. I always had to return the ladder and close the garage door without Henry hearing me.

"He'd get grounded," Tommy continued, "stay in his room all weekend and get stoned, strumming that cheap little guitar he had."

"That Sears acoustic?"

Tommy nodded and smiled, "Man, he killed that piece of shit. Old Henry thought he did Lance a big favor, spending forty-nine dollars on that guitar."

I recalled Lance's torment trying to get a decent guitar. Lance wouldn't dare let Henry know he'd spent money on an electric guitar. Hell, the first year I played with Lance, he didn't own an amplifier, he'd borrow one from somebody or play through Tommy's. For

Lance's eighteenth birthday, Tommy got each of us to pony up sixty-dollars and buy him a used Fender Twin. Lance sat on that same stool in Tommy's garage and just stared at the amp. We never heard a "Thank-You," but for about a month afterward Lance smiled frequently.

Nothing stopped him though, his talent was real. He wasn't a polished singer by any means, yelling as often as he sang. As an instrument player, he was more accomplished than most. Lance's real genius was understanding what worked musically. Which chords in the right progression produced the best listener response. His lyrics were mostly introspective, sad, angst thinly layered over rage and when performed live, he reached people. Most of all, he was obsessed with becoming a star.

One night, I witnessed what only Lance could show his audience. He chose to perform his monster ballad, '*Dream, Darling Dream*' acoustically. He wanted me to provide light background fills, occasional cymbal rolls or fantasy chimes. I went with his flow, watching him soak in the single spotlight, his audience hanging on every note. Every eye traced every move, his face, their breathing in synch with his, every heart hearing Lance. He wasn't another star, he was their star.

It took a couple of years for Lance to accept me and the bass player being the rhythm foundation of every song. Tommy mediated occasional arguments that made rehearsals long and exhausting. Lance didn't like being reminded that he even though he could play, his rhythm wasn't the best. I looked to Tommy, "Remember that night he wanted to fight me when I said he should work in a studio?"

Putting his drink to his lips, Tommy's smile stretched across his face, his laughter spilling into his ginger ale. Time and cigarettes had grooved deep lines at his eyes and the corners of his mouth. Tommy snorted, "Man, he went off, didn't he?"

"Who was that girl with him?" I remembered a bottle blonde who, hearing me call Lance a prick, threw an ashtray across the room, hitting Randy in the back. Lance laughed as she followed with a beer can that spewed foam everywhere. Remembering the kerfuffle Tommy laughed, his head tilted slightly as he held his hand to his lips, "I don't know man. She couldn't throw for shit."

Randy took a spot on the back bench with Tommy and I. The limo swayed from lane to lane as Joey sat alone, looking forward. Watching the clouds slide over the mountains, Randy's eyes searched the horizon before he turned to us, "Who all's going to be at this thing?"

"Well, Lance for sure." Tommy's fingers tapped his glass. "Roger, studio big-shots. Who else?" Turning to me, he stared over his sunglasses again. I sat and thought.

"Darlene called. She's not going to make it," I offered. "Of course, Leslie with her drama."

Leslie was Lance's newest squeeze. At least twenty years younger, they met in rehab. Her life is one drama or disaster after another. She accompanied Lance on this last tour. In the five years between our previous tour and this last one, Lance finally completed rehab. Two other attempts cost the record company one hundred thousand dollars and went nowhere. Each time, Lance walked out after three weeks, way short of the recommended treatment. Relapsing wasn't a question of if, only when?

Randy followed up, "You think anyone from Cactus will show up?"

Joey turned to us, "Cactus? They're coming?"

Cactus Records was the first recording studio to sign us. We were somewhere between an overachieving bar band and a legitimate recording act. We signed the contract one hot, July night in the liquor storage room of a Lincoln Avenue bar in Chicago.

I nudged Tommy, "Wha'dya think? Think they'll show?"

"I don't know, man, that was what? twenty-five, thirty years ago?" We looked to each other, then as if on cue, shook our heads, 'No.'

Lance burned that bridge completely *and* the river it crossed when he called the producer a no-talent hack and the studio manager a fuck-wad. There was a twenty-something kid telling the business people how to record music. I couldn't remember what started the conflict.

"What was that fight about?"

"Who?" Tommy got up an retrieved a second ginger ale.

"Cactus. What started it?"

"Besides Lance calling the owner a fuck-wad?"

"I thought that was the studio manager." Turning back to me, he closed the mini-fridge door, "Yeeaahh, owner *and* studio manager."

I looked to the eastern horizon, the sun still blazing in the west. Tommy came back to the seat, turned, sat and popped his can top all in one motion. Pouring the soda, he exhaled, "Let me think." Finishing the pour, he took a sip and folded his arms across his chest, holding the glass securely in the crook of his left arm.

"Lance wanted to do something behind the glass. Said something like the chorus needed more echo or something. The manager said it was fine and the producer said it sounded great. Lance took off his guitar and tried to get in. The engineer saw him coming and locked the control room door, so, Lance kicked it in."

Tommy shook his head slowly side to side, "After Henry put him in the hospital, he never trusted anybody."

"What?" I tried to remember when they tangled that badly. "When was that?"

"Oh, let me think." Tommy put the glass to his forehead and closed his eyes. "It was when you played with Brad and those guys, '*Monotone*' or something?"

"Monster Tones, jackoff."

Tommy snickered, knowing I hated him making fun of that group. We were bad, no doubt, but he and Lance weren't doing anything. Brad got work at a country club for their Wednesday night, '*Teen Scream*' events. "Henry put him in the hospital?" I asked. Randy leaned over, "What? Henry did what?"

Collecting himself, Tommy waited, hesitant to tell this story. He rubbed his chin, "Henry enrolled Lance in Navy ROTC classes in high school and gave him one hundred and fifty dollars to pay for the uniforms. Lance took the money, bought a new guitar and never went to class. The school sent Henry a letter saying Lance had been dropped from ROTC for excessive absenteeism."

We nod while absorbing information we'd never heard before.

"Then, Lance had a fight with some girl he was seeing, called her a slut. So, one night while Lance was working, the girl's mom brought the new electric and other stuff Lance had left at their house, dropped it all on Henry and Lois and said Lance was never welcomed at their house again."

"How'd that get him to the hospital?"

Tommy bit his lower lip between his teeth, took a deep breath, and exhaled, "Lance was working at the grocery store, remember? Well, he comes home around 10:00, and Henry's waiting for him in the garage. Henry destroys the guitar in front of Lance and he went animal right there." Tommy paused, pinching the bridge of his nose.

Randy looks to Joey and they both shrugged. I sat still, remembering how hard Lance fought to get Henry's permission to work after school and on weekends. People could visit Lance and Beth at their house, but GOD Almighty couldn't convince Henry to let them socialize anywhere else. Trying to fathom how a father could so antagonize his son, I asked, "So, Henry took Lance to the hospital?"

Tommy turned towards to me, "No, the ambulance took Lance to the hospital."

I'm stupefied, I had never heard about this. I pulled down my sunglasses as did Tommy.

"Lois called the fire department after Henry hit Lance so hard, he knocked him out. The emergency room doctor discovered Henry had broken Lance's ribs, and jaw and shattered his cheekbone. That's why he always insisted on being on the left side of the stage. His left cheek was messed up. Drove him nuts."

******

I looked at my watch, in twenty minutes we should be there. We all sit watching cars slip behind as the limo swims past. With the glass partition now raised, the driver's unable to hear us. He's taken off his cap, opened his collar and loosened his tie. Delivering us is his only task today.

"Well," I concluded, "that explains him not going home when Henry died. But he didn't go for his mom either." I looked at the rear wheels of a semi-tractor just outside my little window and wondered, how do you care for someone who once beat you unconscious?

There were months we'd spend apart from one another, glad to be home, alone, going nowhere, doing nothing. We'd reunite to record, swearing this time would be different, professional, fun. A month later we'd all retreated to our comfortable dysfunctions, trapped in the endless creativity for profit hamster-wheel.

Randy pulls me back when he asks loudly, "That wasn't the only time he got his ass kicked. Remember, in Austin, when he tried bringing that groupie to the bus and her husband's standing right next to her?"

Tommy and I nodded, recollecting a night that required five thousand dollars and two cops to save Lance's life. He wanted to fight us both when Tommy called him an idiot. Seeing Lance draw back his left hand in a fist, Tommy spared Lance a disaster, yelling, "Not your chord hand man!"

"Was that the tour after his first rehab?" Joey now joined the conversation.

We sat thinking as a traffic jam slowed the limo to a dead stop. Randy swirls ice cubes in his glass as I sip the last water from my bottle. Before twisting the cap back on, I squeezed the plastic hard, crushing it. "No, that was after the second," I replied, "he came to my house after the first."

My mind went back to Lance's first attempt and escape. He came to my house where he found Linda cleaning the pool. I was recording at Capitol in downtown L.A. and had no idea he'd left the recovery center. Lance and I were friends, sort of, more than acquaintances, less than close. We were band members who enjoyed our mutual success. I didn't offer my hospitality and Lance *never* asked permission. I'm sure he assumed I'd go along with his idea; I always had before and this time shouldn't have been any different. Lance moved in with us for six months, long enough to convince Linda that sleeping with him was better than being married to me.

Linda was exceptionally attractive, having deep mahogany-auburn hair, bright green eyes, full lips and spell-binding legs that flowed smoothly from her cut-off shorts. She laughed with remarkable gusto, confidence and sensual earthiness. She was untethered from any cares when I first met her. Her smile, calling me "Sexy-chops", the sex, all of her was thrilling, I loved her without question or condition.

Lance kept telling me he was writing new material, but I never saw or heard anything. After a while I didn't want to hear anything, by then I'd seen enough. Lance moved into a coach house in Laurel Canyon, catching Linda two or three times a week.

After the divorce was finalized, Linda realized Lance never really loved her. He only wanted her because she was married to me. The following year on tour with my divorce under way, I couldn't figure out which one of them I wanted to kill first.

Lance never worried about me retaliating: he said as much backstage one night. Right before a show started, he sneered, "You'd all be washing dishes if it wasn't for me!"

Silently, we all agreed, none of us had the balls then to think otherwise. Lance was the show, our meal ticket and none of us thought we could succeed without him. Eight hours later I was in a hospital emergency lobby wondering if Linda would survive.

After that night, we waited a year before trying to record again. Tommy and I became solid in friendship and appreciation for one another. But that time away changed our schoolboy allegiance to Lance. We no longer felt insecure without him. During our time off, I accepted that I had become a professional musician, not just in a band. It was how I made my living, the only way I made my living. Wondering if I could cut it with any other musicians, I signed up to work studio sessions with multiple artists. I encountered talent that didn't rely on attitude or anger. I learned not every lead singer was a problem child. At times, I felt conflicted. Studio work was nice, it paid the bills, and I was in my own bed every night. But the laughs, sights, and nights of nailing a live performance from start to finish were dreams come true.

During our rehearsals, Lance could hear things in each member's playing and would openly challenge everyone. Regarding the music, he was usually correct but, his assessments of talent or musicality could be brutal. Sometimes, I was speechless after listening to Lance criticize Tommy. Once, I asked, "Why do you let him talk to you like that?"

Tommy rolled his eyes and looked away, out the studio window, down to the buildings and cars and people below. I asked again, "Tom, seriously, why do you put up with him?"

I watched Tommy absorb a moment where all his avoidance revealed its true value: none. He didn't want to consider choosing between Lance or anything else. Tommy had been able to keep all of us comfortable through humorous distraction or stage spacing. But in this instant, the truth of Lance's toxic and corrosive narcissism confronted him directly. He lit a cigarette and inhaled deeply, taking time to let the smoke sink deep before releasing two streams through his nostrils and speaking the truth.

"Look, you and I know more about Lance than we like. We've seen him at his best and worst. I can't tell you how to live, but I know this: Lance DeMars and all his shit gets me my home in Malibu. He's put more money in my pocket than I ever dreamed possible. Lance is one of the worst human beings I know, working with him is a constant pain in the ass."

He stopped speaking and folded his arms across his chest, looked down to the floor, and quietly finished. "But, I've made my choice to ride this out as long as I can. He can bitch all he wants. He can't play like me, and he knows it. You have to decide what you can accept, man."

Tommy was right, no matter how complicated the rhythm or progression, Lance's left hand was fluid over the fretboard, but, he could only strum chords. Lead playing requires fusing the artist's heart, soul, brain, and coordination, all in the present moment. Lance couldn't get all his parts working in unison. Once, I asked him how he got so good playing chords? He looked to the sky and sighed, "Laying on my bed or standing on a stage. I'm only alive when I'm playing. Every night of my life. I play just for the chance every night."

Some nights, I'd watch Lance and Tommy throw lead riffs back and forth. At first, Tommy kept them simple, but eventually, his creativity would lift off and we could only watch. Lance tried picking lead occasionally. Sometimes he was passable. Some exchanges complimented one another, a bonus for the audience witnessing musical cohesiveness. Tommy continuously worked to improve, his hours on the bus days off in the hotel, over the years, he became a master guitarist. Tommy could throw down superbly for sixty minutes nonstop if he wished. I'm sure some nights he wanted to, but Lance couldn't stand it, so Tommy purposely laid back.

Five years ago, we toured for eight months. Lance was overweight, sluggish and generally a pain in everyone's ass. We were miserable and it showed in every performance for the entire tour. I remember thinking we'd run our course and could no longer draw large crowds to satisfy the label or ourselves.

Just before our last show, Tommy and Lance had a massive blow-up backstage. For the next three hours that night, I watched them trying to jam their anger up each other's asses in front of sixteen thousand burned-out, middle-aged ghosts, trying to relive their youth. Two mediocre encores followed and then it was over. No band member spoke to any other for the next six months. It was heavenly.

******

The limo slows for the exit ramp to our final performance. A week ago, this show was unthinkable, today it's a fact, clear and precise. Once more, Stonecraft would please fans, giving a lasting memory perfectly choreographed to milk every emotion. Now, we're caught in urban traffic, stop-and-go, lights and crosswalks. It's our final approach, and it's a crawl, just like Lance's last attempt at sobriety, starting when he fell out of the limo in the studio parking lot.

No one picked him up, so he crawled into the lobby screaming, slobbering, collapsing in front of the receptionist's desk. Roger Corman, tour manager and studio exec producing our album ran around, yelling, "Call an ambulance! Call an ambulance!"

The press reported Lance suffered from exhaustion. We all knew better, nobody slips into a coma from being tired. Four months later Tommy and I were in Cabo, watching Sammy Hagar run the show when Roger called requesting a meeting in Studio Three. The following Monday, we arrived at two o'clock in the afternoon,

110

completely disinterested in anything. Joey had been working in the studio with some new talent and Randy was hunting elk or something in Wyoming. Nobody expected to see Lance, nobody really wanted to.

Instead of going to the studio, Roger brought us into a conference room. There at one end of the giant mahogany table, sat Lance. I didn't recognize him at first. He'd lost about forty pounds, his hair was shorter, and he'd shaved off his beard, if you could call it that. He was looking out the fifth-floor window, staying silent until Roger asked him to join us. Pale and quiet, his hands trembled slightly opening a bottle of water. He never looked directly at me. I thought I was seeing a ghost.

I was simultaneously disgusted and intrigued. Decades of drugs and alcohol had flowed through those veins and internal organs. Even through the tinted window's light, his wrinkly skin looked almost transparent, no stronger than tissue paper.

"Lance," Tommy smiled, extending his hand to shake, "How you doin' man?"

I couldn't believe it, Tommy acting like we're at a class reunion.

"I'm, …. I'm okay, man. How bout' you?"

"I'm good, I'm good." The smile continued under nodding. Then I noticed Tommy's eyes as he pulled down his sunglasses. They were narrowed, like doing an interview for some unknown magazine. He was so uncertain, his banter light, upbeat, nothing of substance.

Lance looked toward my seat, and nodded once. I returned one nod, there, we'd said enough.

"Tom, Tim," Roger sat at the head of the table, "Guys, I called you here, because, well, as you can see, Lance is back."

I watched Roger struggle to figure out which of us would be the hardest sell. A stubby little man with a round, balding head, his wispy goatee only made his expansive forehead more noticeable. He tried to look relaxed in his pale, yellow golf shirt and grey polyester slacks. A rectangular linked gold bracelet on one wrist and oversized gold wristwatch on the other, a gold pinky-ring with a red stone completed his parasitic appearance. The worn black loafers with foam soles and yellow socks only made his aura more superficial. Sitting still for a moment, he interlocked his fingers, crossing his thumbs, staring intently like he was about to confess every sin he's ever committed. "He's fully completed the program at Victory Wellness Center. He's been attending meetings, uh, what meetings you going to Lance?"

"Oh man, NA, AA, Progressive Healing," he stopped and stared at the tabletop. Then, without looking up, took a deep breath and coughed, "There's others I can't remember right now."

Bullshit, I knew better. I had witnessed night after night on tour, even stoned senseless, Lance remembered every chord progression, every lyric perfectly, for twenty or thirty songs.

"Right, right." Roger turned to us and opened his hands, palms up, his eyes soft, "You see, he's made it. Lance has turned over a new leaf, hah, I mean a new life!"

I looked to Tommy, his head never moving. I sat back in my chair and Roger continued. "Look, I think we can take Lance's wonderful success and, with your help, of course, and you too Tim, put together a whole new package of Stonecraft music. Of course, we'll need to coordinate the release with a tour schedule, but I think your fans are craving, and salivating at the idea of new music and a tour. And with Lance recovered, he'll have an even *bigger* audience, right?"

Tommy slouched back, wove his fingers together over his belt buckle and pursed his lips. Reclining in his chair, Lance folded his arms across his chest. *'Oh boy,'* I thought, *'here we go.'*

Roger's head switched back and forth, right to left and back, perspiration had added a sheen to his forehead and pate. I had nothing to say, not that anyone asked, *thank you*. Keeping with past practice,

Lance thought the moment was his. He sat up and put both forearms on the table, "Look, I know things didn't end too well with us Tom."

"They ended just fine, Lance. You went your way and I went mine."

"Yeah. But the tour was successful."

"Yeah, you got your thirty-five percent, the label got thirty and we got to split what was left. One more time, we got crapped on."

Roger tried turning down the flames, "Tom listen, this is the last album under that contract. If you want, we'll do this one, then sit down and write a totally new deal. One that you'll like, okay?"

Tommy looked to me, his smile devilishly wide, *"Whad'youu think Tim, you happy with six percent?"*

I side-eyed Tom as my stomach knotted, he knew better. He turned back to Roger, "Tim's got two kids from his first marriage, remember Lance? They'll be going to college soon."

Lance rolled his eyes, "Psshhh" and sank back into his chair. Tom turned full on to Roger, placed his hands on the tabletop palms down and leaned forward. "Roger, I got three kids, a mortgage, a wife who wants to finish college, a bad back and arthritis in both hands. I talked to my lawyer: we've completed this contract. This last recording is an option everyone has to sign on to. I'm not signing for the same money."

Lance bolted upright, barking, "I knew he'd screw it up!"

Roger stared at Tommy, his eyes large, straining in their sockets. I remember watching, waiting, preparing myself to pull Tommy off Roger or Lance, thinking to myself, *Hell, He might take em' both.'*

Lance mounted another charge, "Look, everybody knows Stonecraft doesn't work unless *ALL* of us are in. You, me, Timmy, the whole band. We record, we tour, we bag a ton of money, just like before."

"No," I shot to Lance, "you bagged a ton, we got shit."

His head snapped to me, surprised by my speaking up, siding with Tom. Raising one hand to his chin, he waited, watching for who would speak next. We stared at each other for ten seconds as the room's air condensed before us. We all waited, unsure what could be said, what would be heard.

Lance stared at the tabletop. Tommy sat back, and locked both hands behind his head before turning away from Roger to look out the windows. I let my left-hand finger roll over the tabletop, over and over and over. Almost laid out across the chair, Lance's eyes were slits and his breathing slow. After three or four horrible minutes, Roger caved, "Tom, Tim, what do you want in a new deal?"

Tom looked at me, his arms still suspended, "It's got to be equal, for everybody, otherwise, we're wasting our time."

Roger nodded, "Of course, of course."

"Equal authorship and performance rights on all new material." Tom looked straight at Lance, "No more single artist shit."

Roger pulled out a notepad and pen, scribbling while he nodded, "Sure, we all want that. Don't we, Lance?" Lance didn't move a muscle. I remembered thinking he'd fallen asleep. Tom leaned in my direction, bringing my attention back to the conversation. "What about you, Tim? What do you want?"

My eyes searched the tabletop before a long-held stream of frustration seasoned with dreams poured out. "Lance, I don't know if you can cut it anymore, man. I mean, look atcha', you're barely alive. You need us as much, hell, more than we need you."

I looked to Tommy, then to Roger. Tommy nodded in agreement ever so subtly. Like his mouth, Roger's face hung open, eyes blank, his brain frozen. I took a deep breath and then looked back to Lance. "But we all know how to make this worthwhile. I think we should record, complete the tour, then take thirty days off, sit down and divide the net proceeds equally."

Roger's head recoiled, and his hand stopped above the notepad. I watched his brain working hard, trying to think. Surveying the table, he saw Tom looking smug, Lance may or may not be listening and I had spoken up for the first time. Confused, wanting the recording and tour, he had to agree, he had to give us what we wanted. Lance DeMars with different musicians was a nuclear holocaust and Stonecraft without Lance DeMars was worthless.

******

Joey called out to Tommy, "Our gear's there, right? Do we have to sound check?"

Looking out the door window, Tommy nodded before signaling the driver to drop the glass partition. As it slid down, he answered, "No, no sound check, just do the numbers. Ask him how much longer?"

Joey scooted along the short seat and leaned into the partition close to the driver. He waited while the driver checked his phone and the limo's mapping system. Nodding his head, Joey lifts one hand, waving into the rearview mirror before turning back to us.

"Fifteen minutes at least, traffic's a mess."

Fifteen more minutes, one show and we all go home. I think back to the first night of this circus six months ago. The record had been out for eight weeks, getting mixed reviews and sluggish sales. Tommy and I thought we'd overplayed our hand. Lance was workable, smartly choosing to abandon any thoughts of playing any lead. His hand and mind coordination were still hit-and-miss. I asked Tommy, "What'd you think after the show in Baltimore?"

"This year?"

"Yeah,"

"I thought we were lucky we didn't get booed off the stage."

Tommy could read a crowd better than anyone I knew. I thought back to how at first, Lance struggled with the simplest songs. His perspiration soaked everything, and he gasped between songs like he was running a marathon. I tended to suck in the first fifteen minutes, never sure I could feel Randy's downbeat. For the first time in a long time, I had doubts.

"This traffic's messing everything up. Think everybody will wait?" Randy looked worried. Tommy smiled, staring ahead, "Relax, they'll wait. Lance is not doing anything without us."

I thought back to the second show, Richmond, Virginia. We were better, rough, but better. Nobody talked before we warmed up. A silent quintet, the mood somber in the dressing room, like waiting in a doctor's lobby. The tour progressed over highways, stages and weeks, but we each remained isolated. Six months of one-nighters can be a flash or slow walk to the electric chair. The band holds the dice. I looked out the opera window and asked, "What'd you think at San Diego?"

Tommy waited, his face down, sunglasses slightly forward. I watched his eyes examine multiple thoughts. He folded his arms over his chest, "I thought he'd finally come out of whatever he couldn't handle."

Tom's assessment was understandable even if mistaken. Lance was performing, not just going through the motions. His voice got stronger, and his hands showed some flexibility. He stayed in tune and rhythm with me and Randy when Tommy or Joey soloed. Before I could speak, Tom added, "Of course, now we know why."

Over the tour, as Lance got more comfortable, I sensed some collision lurking ahead. Then, last Thursday, our tour finale in San Diego delivered the ghost. Lance walked out on stage last, smiling, upbeat, strapped on his guitar and plugged in before blasting, '*Night of Danger*' like twenty years earlier. Lance had come out to kick the audience's ass from the first note. The entire show flowed, we flew from one hit to another. The crowd roared, singing along, shouting choruses, and cheering themselves hoarse. Lance kept looking to us all, frequently saying, "Ride the lighting, boys!" We gave three encores for the first time ever. Before the last one, Lance told us, "Just follow me, guys."

We took our places as the crowd cheered, roaring and whistling, fueling an energy rush of over 100,000 volts. I remembered feeling not the least bit tired, even after being on stage for almost three hours. Lance strutted up to the microphone and announced, "All right, kids, this is what it's all about."

For the next twenty minutes we grooved, '*Johnny Be Good*' leaving the audience wet, spent, and delirious. Coming off the stage, Roger greeted us, smiling like he'd just won the lottery, "Great show, guys, you killed it. I mean absolutely killed it."

Making sure to shake all our hands, I noticed his sweaty palms. Tommy wiped his hand on his pants without saying a word. Joey looked at Randy, and they busted out laughing. Roger cornered Lance by a stairway railing leading to a hall under the main floor.

Roger was euphoric, "Lance, get everybody back to the hotel, the press is waiting, and I mean a lot of 'em." Lance nodded his head and stood on the top stair. Needing a shower and a change of clothes, I went to the dressing room. Thirty minutes later, as I was drying my hair, Tom stood in the shower area doorway, "You going over there?"

"Yeah, why not? We make our appearance, eat, get something to drink and split. We're done, you know?"

Tom nodded, a toothpick in his teeth, which he starts using to one side of his mouth, "You seen Lance?"

"Here?"

He nodded again as the toothpick came out.

"Nah, I haven't seen him since we walked off stage."

Tom turned to the main room, "Randy, where's Lance?"

Randy looked to Joey, the two girls with him and back to Tom, "I dunno."

"Did he leave already?" I wonder aloud.

Randy heard me and yelled back, "The limo's still outside, so, he didn't take that. Did he leave with Roger?"

"Roger's still backstage, talking to people," Tom replied. A moment passed then we both looked to each other. My breathing shortened, my stomach started tightening, and the collision is happening. Tom's face morphed to weary adulthood as he asked, "Where'd you see him last?"

I dropped the towel on the counter, "C'mon with me."

We walked out of the room as Randy and Joey watched. I took Tom to the stairway. No one was there. I started walking down as Tom said, "I'm gonna check the stage, maybe he's with Roger."

Five steps down to a landing, then I turned a one-eighty for five more. At the bottom, a cinder block hallway to the right channels everyone toward two large grey steel doors at its end. Hazard warnings regarding extreme voltage brazenly snagged my attention. Three doors on the hall's left side bore worn signage. Two were restrooms separated by a utility closet.

Seeing the 'Men's' sign, I pushed the door open. Opposite the doorway, under a mirror on a light grey wall, a white sink waited. The paper towel dispenser directed your vision back to the partition immediately to the door's right, where behind it, the single white urinal hung. Further to the right, a metal stall hid a toilet. I walked in, and viewed the sink, urinal and a lowly wastebasket. In the silence of my suspicions, a groan rolled from under the toilet partition out to my feet.

Cautiously, I stepped over to the stall's metal door. Standing close, I slowly pushed it open. My vision narrowed and I lifted my eyes from the floor to view the collision. My body flushed numb as the image overwhelmed me. On the toilet, under the callous glare of two sixty-watt fluorescent bulbs, slumped against the wall on the toilet paper holder, Lance was unconscious.

His belt sagged above a needled syringe that hung from the inner crease of his right arm. His eyes closed, head tilted slightly upward, and his torso held its position. The paltry lighting accentuated his pasty complexion and blue lips. A small bead of foam pouched in the left corner of his mouth. His jaw was slack, and his tongue was visible above his lower teeth. This was bad, this was too much. This was the status quo.

The bathroom door swung open as Tom came through. Stopping after two steps, he looked to me, silent, suspecting. I shrugged, exhaled long and slow, then nodded towards Lance and stepped back to the sink. Tom walked to the stall door, pushed it open, "Are you FUCKING KIDDING ME?!"

He stepped back, placing his hands on his hips, "How long you think he been like this?"

"Twenty minutes, at least."

"Should we tell Roger?" Tommy asked me, staring at Lance.

"What's he gonna do?"

Tom stood thinking, his face swaying from tortured to disgusted and back. He stared at the form on the toilet and asked, "Did you know?"

"I suspected."

"How long?"

"Last two or three weeks. I saw the demon again."

"How'd I miss it?"

I almost laughed out loud, "Tom, you didn't want to see it."

"No. You're right. I thought he got it. Thought he'd finally changed."

I looked to the sink, spying a matchbook, laying aside a twist-off bottle cap and three charred, spent matches. I glanced to the wastebasket, where a small translucent envelope lay atop some used paper towels. "He was never gonna change man." I summarized, "This was his dream."

Tom stayed motionless as my words seeped through his heart and mind, down into his gut. Turning his head slightly to me, he processed forty years of ongoing tension, conflict and brilliance. "You think he wanted this?"

"I don't think he ever saw it in a hole like this." I looked to the burnt matches, "But, he was always looking for it."

Tom walked from the stall to the opposite wall. He leaned back against it as he sunk his hands into his blazer pockets. Once more, part of his youth slipped away. He sees it, and knows it, but can't understand how it happened without his permission. Silently, Tom and I accepted this inevitable destruction. We'd watched Lance rehearse it over and over for forty years. Your demons only survive if you keep breathing life into them, so much for a successful tour.

In almost a whisper, Tom asked, "Think he'll make it?"

"I don't know." I thought of all the doubts we'd fought. My mind chopped and churned through all the years, the fights, the disconnects, betrayals, suspicions, frustrations. Henry's bullshit and Lance's self-destructive compulsions. And for what? I let my thoughts run like water down a hillside, "And I really don't care."

Tom stared at the floor, waiting, wondering. I wondered too, what does it take for someone to stop fighting their life? When would enough be enough? How much was needed to fill something that had no bottom?

Again, in almost a whisper, Tom brought voice to the moment, "What do you think we should do?"

"What 'we' Tom?" I was numb to any more drama, any more crises. I couldn't accept another problem involving Lance and its effect on my life. "What about him? What should he have done?" I shook my head and resigned, "I'm done."

"You're leaving?" Tom asked, his eyes wide with surprise. "He's our friend man, since high school."

"Tom, for forty years, we've let Lance be Lance, no matter how it felt. Tonight's no different. You knew him, back in your dads' garage, on the road, in the studio. Hell, he took us all for the ride. But that?" I pointed to the stall. "That's not our friend from high school. That's a grown man who couldn't accept it coming to an end for him, so he quit."

"You think this is his idea? Just bailing out tonight?

"This, here tonight, this was Lance's ultimate jerking us off. He did this himself, not us. And if it didn't end this way tonight, he would've kept at it until it did. Tom, Lance never came back, he quit on us years ago."

Tom watched me start toward the door. As I passed him, he looked once more toward Lance, then followed me out. We returned to the backstage area where Roger was still laughing, gesturing, smiling, clueless. We turned and went to the parking lot, the limo idling as Joey and Randy waited. Tom asked, "You guys ready?"

"Where's Lance?" Randy asked, looking to the stage door.

I walked into the cool night air, towards the limo's open door, "I guess he found his own ride."

******

We slowly line up with other limos entering the cemetery, inching caterpillar-like towards a setting at the graveyard's back boundary. A silver coffin sits on a platform covered with purple fabric. A temporary canopy offers seating for family and close friends. Other than his sister Beth, Lance had neither.

To the west of the canopy, under a spreading oak tree, a low riser holds my drums. Behind two microphones and Joe's keyboard, three amplifiers wait. Racks hold Tommy's guitar and Randy's bass. First, we'll do '*Save My Heart*', Lance's first hit and then '*Cradle My Love*, the current hit that made this tour worthwhile.

Our limo finally stops, and we crawl out. Randy leads, Joey follows Tom before I step out to a crowd of two or three hundred people. I paused to view the balloons, signs, phones taking pictures and hand-held bouquets. Mascara lines down teenage cheeks imitate their mother's pained grimaces. People waited quietly as we walked in unison, sunglasses on, coats buttoned, faces solemn. This is where Stonecraft ends, forty years beyond the Times Lounge. The weight of memories pulls each step forward, slowly, deliberately. I wonder if any of us will remember anything with affection?

The terrain slopes up to the gravesite, and a breeze blows through the trees. Surreal relief lies ahead in this lost corner of Los Angeles. I look up to see my life, the travels, rehearsals, boredom, elation and disbelief, wrapped in a silver casket. Lance DeMars got me here and now he's gone, never to be seen again. I'm relieved and I'm lost. The force that gave me a dream, success and comfort is no more. The agony of that force is also gone, and emptiness swirls within me instead.

At twenty paces from the coffin, I stop, the weight of forty years filling my chest. My legs weakened, I shudder, my head clouded, heavy. I wanted many different things at many different times, I never wanted anything like this. My breaths are deep, and labored. I'm stopped, a heaviness filling me. I feel Tom wrap his arm over my shoulders as he whispers "C'mon man, It's almost over."

Genetic Anguish

G. E. Russell

I still fight dragons of doubt and self-censure, chasing my belief in redemption through selflessness. I've had to make myself from memories and impressions of what my father and grandfather weren't. Two years after my father's death, my son was born. Life pushed me to the other side of generational drama. I had no resources on fathering a son, no trail guide or paternal consigliere to advise me. My anguish sometimes flames late at night, searing me with anger and shame.

Late one Saturday in May 1969, around 6:30 pm, from the living room, I heard the back doorbell's metallic notes announce a visitor's presence. I walked into the kitchen and looked through the screen door to a waiting silhouette. Once closer, my pace slowed as I recognized the smaller man wearing a pastel short-sleeved shirt and belted, double-reverse pleated dress slacks. The flat, open collar revealed his wife-beater and some silver chest hairs, his jaw set, and a half-completed cigar tucked in his mouth's right corner. Clean-shaven, clip-on sunglass lenses covered his eyes under his light blue fedora's brim. His shoulders angled down to sleeve hems hanging loosely over the still muscular but senescent arms, patiently controlling each hand's waiting suitcase. I recognized the form instantly, if only remotely, from many years earlier, during my summer visits to Chicago when we played catch every day. Cautiously, I asked, "Grandpa?"

Before he could respond through the screen, my father stepped from behind me and down one step to the backdoor landing. Twisting the door handle, surprise-filled my father's greeting, "Dad, what are you doing here?"

"I'm moving in," the visage replied.

Pushing the door open, my father stood erect. I watched the two men silently pass within inches of each other, never stopping to shake hands, hug or smile. My grandfather walked through the kitchen and into our living room. Once in its center, he lowered the two suitcases, placed his hands on his hips and exhaled slowly, his cigar exhaust announcing his arrival. Again, my father passed me, "Moving in? What happened to the house in Missouri?"

"Ah, I sold it. That was your mother's house, Jimmy. I couldn't live there anymore."

'Jimmy' was my father, forty-six years old, a decorated veteran of two wars. Taller, and more muscular than Grandpa, now married with two kids. 'Jim' as he preferred to be called, was a mortgage holder in a middle-class suburban neighborhood. But to his family, he was always his childhood name, 'Jimmy', a demotion my father hated.

"Sold it? You sold the house?" Incredulity animated my father, "What about the furniture?"

"Sold it with the house."

My mother appeared from her bedroom, "Why, hello Jim." Looking to my grandfather quizzically, she asked, "What brings you here?" She eyed my father suspiciously, uncertainty or spontaneity being verboten in my mother's world.

"Dad sold the house in Missouri, he's, … he's, …"

"Movin' in," Grandpa asserted, turning back to my father, "Just like when you were a kid, over the grocery store, remember?"

"Dad, that was the Depression."

His face expressionless, he waited for our acquiescence. He didn't suffer ambiguity or uncertainty either. His life had always been doing what he wanted, when he wanted, how he wanted, no questions, explanations, or second guesses. Once long ago, a snappy dresser and neighborhood Zeus just south of the Stockyards, he'd survived extravagant and tragic times, including five years in the Joliet Men's Correctional Facility. At holiday tables, his early life was family mythology. Other men in the family subordinated themselves, he never offered or admitted anything. Now, in his eighth decade's latter half, he unilaterally decided he'd finish life with us. The world conformed to the will of James Thomas Russell Himself, or it simply didn't exist.

"Well," Mom stammered, "well, you can take the bedroom next to the bathroom."

And just like that, my late teens were resolved to a bedroom in the finished lower level.

Grandpa quietly emptied the contents of the suitcase into either the drawers or the dresser top before walking back from the bedroom to the living room. Strolling through the kitchen, past the dining area and into the family room, he silently examined our ranch-style home. His eyes noted window locations, the streets making the corner we lived on, everything strategically identified and mentally cataloged.

An hour later, a Saturday dinner of grilled hamburgers, baked beans and potato chips awaited us on the kitchen table. He came, sat in the chair my mother usually occupied, and silently waited to be served. We sat still as Dad said grace, the only time I would hear my father pray aloud, and then dinner began.

Taking a slice of onion and putting it on top of his burger, he then dribbled mustard from the plastic vial on his bun's lower half. I still enjoy that combination today.

To reduce the tension, my father tried multiple queries, like when did He leave Missouri?

"This morning."

My mother also attempted polite conversation, "How was the driving, Jim?"

"Horseshit."

Silently I watched, captivated by the dynamics unfolding, seeing my parent's obvious discomfort with this inscrutable presence sitting before them.

We finished the meal but unlike other nights, there was no twenty-to-thirty-minute conversation afterward to enhance the digestion of food or the day. Everyone arose, quietly clearing the table, everyone but him. He walked into the family room and directly to the sofa's far end. This was closest to the bay window that looked out to the street, a vantage point to watch vehicular or pedestrian traffic hidden by shadows of reflected daylight. It was where my mother liked to sit while she and my father watched television. But again, he staked out new territory, drawing his boundary line, announcing the start of the passive-aggressive dance he and my mother would vivify for years.

For the next six days I carefully kept my distance between my father and grandfather. I watched the two silverbacks move about, silently posturing, aware of each other's presence, feigning their alpha primacy disinterest. Their personal war began following Grandpa's five-year incarceration. Shortly after Grandpa was released, my father lied about his age and enlisted in the Navy. Neither man ever spoke of that time, in fact, they didn't speak to each other about anything in their past.

The household daily routine streamlined the tensions. My father left for work before Grandpa came to the table for morning coffee. Later, he'd leave and walk to a shopping center, eight blocks away, where he spent most of the day reading the paper, drinking coffee, and watching. Dinner became a ritual: Dad's prayer, quiet eating, then cleanup and leaving. One night there was a brief, terse exchange between him and my father regarding money. Sitting at the large round table in one corner of our family room, my father's bi-weekly practice of paying bills and watching television was encroached upon by Him watching a baseball game. Trying to demonstrate fealty, I cautiously asked my father in the hallway, out of Grandpa's earshot, "Why don't you tell him to turn the TV down?"

Biting the corner of his lip, my father anxiously looked to the family room, "Listen, one time I saw him knock a guy out with one punch. That old Mick could kick both our asses if he wanted to."

I thought instantly to a Saturday afternoon three years earlier. I'd almost completed the list of tasks my father handed me at breakfast. He'd finished his work and was sitting in the family room, about to eat a simple lunch sandwich, chips, and pickle while watching a baseball game. My fifteen-year-old's narcissistic complaint landed on his ears as he swallowed some beer. Putting the can on the coffee table, he stood and beckoned me to follow. Once outside, behind the garage, in traditional Irish-American fashion, he turned and lifted his fists, saying, "Let's go."

I presented my boxing form and quickly landed an overhand right on his chin, snapping his head sideways only to see it return, eyes focused directly on mine. Before I could blink, a lightning-quick left jab to my forehead brought a strong right fist into my diaphragm. I collapsed, unable to breathe or think. Minutes later, I returned to the family room where my father sat calmly watching the game, eating his sandwich like nothing ever happened. I never challenged him again.

Four more weeks of the new dance continued with only my sister being comfortable, sitting immediately to Grandpa's left at dinner, asking him questions, smiling, laughing at his answers. Reconsidering my father's apprehension, I didn't feel that confident. One night my doubts were reinforced when the evening news reported the death of 'Mo Mo' Giancana. Sitting in his sofa perch, Grandpa snickered, looked briefly to my father, then got up and walked out to the deck. My father looked to me, his eyes flashing, "What'd I tell ya?"

A new tension between my mother and father became palpable, in short, whispered exchanges. Mom distrusted Dad's family and believed my father's deference was a sign of weakness. She thought she understood the dysfunction between my father and Grandpa, but now she watched it bloom in real time, full of grievance, ache and subdermal rage. My grandfather was an intermittent presence throughout my father's life. Now, this resurrected malaise presaged open warfare.

June progressed with my mother, father and I leaving for work early each morning. Occasionally, tense exchanges between Grandpa and my father boiled to decibel levels alerting us all. Voices hissed and snarled in snappish whispers, flashing eyes, a cigar between two fingers bobbing up and down, emphasizing a decision. Grandpa developed his routine, his acquaintances at the shopping center, living out his days, a widower waiting to die.

A virulent skirmish between them erupted one Friday night right before dinner. Fourth of July was Saturday, meaning Friday required preparations for cookouts, parade watching, and fireworks. Nobody heard exactly what was said on the deck, but once Grandpa completed dinner, he went to his room for the rest of the night. Saturday morning, he washed, shaved, ate breakfast and left. Not one word spoken by anyone to anyone.

The sun blistered the day at ninety-five degrees under a cloudless, burning sky. My father mowed the front and back yards. My mother shopped, and I left for something I could enjoy. Returning home, Mom and I found Dad out on the deck, his face, arms, torso, and legs all a boiled lobster red. Sitting in the chaise lounge next to my father was our neighbor Harry, almost as drunk. The small redwood table between them held an empty Johnny Walker bottle and an ashtray brimming with ashes and multiple crushed butts. Shortly after we arrived, my father and Harry decided to play tennis on the middle school courts, five minutes away by car, and twelve walking. They left as the sun, descending to the west, still mercilessly baked the earth.

I was hungry. My mother asked me to start the grill. Thinking about the two inebriates, I felt disgust and loathing for something I couldn't identify. The charcoal fell loudly into the grill basin before I generously sprayed lighter fluid about. One match sent a flame six feet above my head, black smoke signaling a dreadful meal's beginning. As the briquettes slowly changed from black to silver-white, my mother made a salad.

"How long do you think they'll be gone?" I asked her.

"They'll be back, probably less than an hour."

"You gonna wait to make dinner?"

"Did you light the coals?" Mom asked me.

"Yeah,"

"How long can they wait?"

"Maybe a half-hour, forty-five minutes." I shrugged.

"Let's wait a half-hour. If your father's not back, we'll go ahead and eat."

I lounged on the sofa, its only occupant for the first time in weeks. Twenty minutes after my father's departure, the back screen door slapped against its jamb. Grandpa walked into the kitchen and pulled a six-pack of beer out of a brown bag, his bicep knotting up, the size of a baseball as he held the cans. Saying nothing, he opened the refrigerator door and pushed things around until the cans fit neatly in the top shelf's center. After loading the refrigerator, he went to his room and closed its door.

Five minutes later, just as my mother entered the family room, my father came through the same screen door. She turned and went into the kitchen, "Hi, ready to eat?"

My father tilted slightly left, hands on hips, sweat running down his face, dripping off the tip of his nose. "Is he here?" Nodding her head, she pressed her lips together before softly confiding, "He's in his room."

Hearing my father's voice, I stood up, not sure of my next move. Standing still in the family room, I watched them over my mother's shoulder. My father looked out the double windows, across the yard to the garage. His right hand came to his nose, thumb to one side, fingers to the other, covering his mouth, he pinched and held, breathing deeply. Turning away, he walked slowly through the kitchen and living room, down the hallway to the bedroom door.

Two knocks were followed by the door's opening. My father's voice came first, then a lower response, indiscernible to me. Some further talk, short exchanges before I clearly heard, "Fine." The door closed and my father returned to the kitchen, "He says he's not hungry."

"I bought a steak just for him."

"He said he's not hungry."

"Should I cook the steak, in case he changes his mind?"

"Jean, he does a lot of shit, but he doesn't change his mind."

There it was, the line drawn between them about him. My mother was determined to continue our lives despite Grandpa's presence; my father wanted anything but that. The dinner table was prepared while I tended three steaks on the grill. My father sat on his chaise lounge, staring across our backyard to the empty field beside St. Bridget's Church parking lot. Even besotted, my father's mind churned fitfully. He pounded down a bottle of beer, not one of the cans, staring to the distant blue sky above rooftops, evergreens, and leafy trees. Occasionally, birds flitted by, landing on telephone lines running to the pole at our backyard's corner. Drinking his beer, my father watched them come and go.

We sat down to eat, my father in his seat, my mother in mine, and I in my sister's. The fourth chair sat empty, my sister was at a friend's house. We ate quietly and tried making relevant conversation despite my father's limited awareness. Alcohol, mixed with searing heat and resurgent emotions, reduced my father to a silent, withdrawn captive.

Suddenly, Grandpa entered the kitchen and walked directly to the refrigerator. He retrieved a sixteen-ounce can of his beer, standing upright before striding boldly past the table. He proceeded out to the deck, the cylinder's hush softly completing the screen door's closing.

Sniffing loudly, my father almost choked. I looked to him sitting in his chair, the evening sunlight streaming through the double windows behind him, illuminating all air and pouring over his rounded shoulders. Head bowed, my father's hands curled together in his lap as his body quaked, tears rolling down his cheeks. I felt empty and disoriented, a confusing vacuum swallowing my being. I'd seen my father weep just once before, the day we buried his mother. That sorrow came from the heart, a loss justifying pity and indulgence. These tears bore consternation, and dismay, incapable of soothing pain. Now sobbing came forth from the man to my left, his lower lip extended, eyes closed. Her contempt unleashed, my mother sat back and ruthlessly asked, "Have all your fears come back to haunt you?"

Dad's shaking continued as we all sat in the stale, dry, sunlit air. I watched my father sink into boyhood distrust and confusion. As I struggled, his head nodded and he softly cried, "I don't know what to do."

The fading sunlight pulled me to my left, towards my father, my body ignoring my soul's urge to extend my arm to his, to comfort gently, to voice, "It's alright, Dad, it's alright."

But I didn't. I couldn't. I too was afraid.

Locked in my emotional paralysis, I silently watched the strongest man I'd ever known sitting in tears, reduced to a blubbering child. I felt his self-respect melting before us, his dignity pouring forth, covering the table. I wanted to help, to console and soothe his disfigured heart. But I was too deeply trapped within myself by emotions and misgivings that, regardless of age, bleed men of their self-confidence.

The following spring, unable to watch these two demi-gods and their emotional, tectonic, wrestling any longer, I left. A year of hitch-hiking was followed by a Selective Service letter that compelled my four-year enlistment. Three years after discharge, after playing college football, spending life and energy wantonly, searching to find myself, I was seated next to a hospital bed, alone, watching my grandfather lay in sheets, tubes, wires and the soft beeps of small machines. My mother had called me, saying he wasn't doing well. He drifted in and out of consciousness while I waded through guilt and confusion. We never spoke, I wasn't certain he knew I was there. Sometime later that night he died. Standing next to his casket at the funeral home, I cried openly, unable to see my life without his presence. My father and mother dutifully returned him to my grandmother, his beloved Ruth, burying him next to her in Missouri.

Three more years passed, and I again sat alone next to another bedridden dying man, my father. Again, my brain stumbled and reeled while my mouth remained locked. I couldn't acknowledge death hovering over him, his body emaciated by pancreatic cancer, booze, loneliness and fear. He laid on a bed provided by hospice workers in my sister's bedroom, thanking them repeatedly for their care, their smiles and understanding cooed with practiced compassion. I sat mute, another piece of furniture with Dad's nightstand, pitcher, and glass. Once again, I was away when the final moment came. Once again, I stood through a visitation, next to an open coffin holding someone that resembled my heritage, something vague but intriguing.

For years, I struggled to accept they were both dead, gone forever, with no chance for anyone to reconcile anything. I was alone with questions and doubts and confusion, charred by indeterminable loss. No fraternal joy from a shared perspective or appreciation. No laughter over memorable mistakes or personal triumphs. I have only one photograph of the three of us together, a grainy image of three males standing side by side, a visible distance between each, smiling to the camera but not touching one another. Once we lived together, those lives are now distant memories.

So, I pray daily for the strength and courage to respond to my son for anything, any time. I believe in his self-confidence to confront me, to demand, if necessary, whatever he needs to be whole. I promise myself when he does, I'll be approachable, accountable, and honest. But he may never ask. And I will understand.

www.ingramcontent.com/pod-product-compliance
Lightning Source LLC
Chambersburg PA
CBHW040831010826
48978CB00012BB/700